Center for Basque Studies
Basque Literature Series, No. 3

BASQUE LITERATURE SERIES

RAMON SAIZARBITORIA

Rossetti's Obsession

Translated from Basque by
Madalen Saizarbitoria

Basque Literature Series Editors
Mari Jose Olaziregi and Linda White

Center for Basque Studies
University of Nevada, Reno

Center for Basque Studies
Basque Literature Series, No. 3

Center for Basque Studies
University of Nevada, Reno
Reno, Nevada 89557
http://basque.unr.edu

Library of Congress Cataloging-in-Publication Data

Saizarbitoria, Ramón.
  [Rossetti-ren obsesioa. English]
  Rossetti's obsession / Ramon Saizarbitoria ; translated from Basque
by Madalen Saizarbitoria.
     p. cm. -- (Basque literature series ; no. 3)
  Summary: "A humorous novel about an insecure writer's efforts to
retrieve a note he once sent to a woman, which caused her to fall in
love with him. He hopes that the note will have the same effect on his
new romantic interest"--Provided by publisher.
  ISBN 1-877802-60-3 (pbk.) -- ISBN 1-877802-61-1 (hardcover)
  I. Saizarbitoria, Madalen. II. Title. III. Series.

PH5339.S16R6713 2006
899'.923--dc22
                                        2006000510

The Center for Basque Studies wishes to gratefully acknowledge the generous financial support of the Government of the Basque Autonomous Community for the publication of this book.

RAMON SAIZARBITORIA

Rossetti's Obsession

I put the manuscript back in the envelope in which it had been sent and lingered at the window, staring out at the gray foam-specked sea, which seemed enraged under the weight of the black sky. This sight alone would have been enough to make the feeling of wetness cut straight to my bones, but the house itself was also very damp from having stood empty so long. To make matters worse, I hadn't been able to get the heating to work, despite several attempts. However, I knew it was the thought of never seeing Victoria again that caused me to feel ill at ease and made me shiver on that harsh autumn morning.

"We'll meet again," she said before leaving and added "someday" after a short pause. The response is crystal clear to anybody who wants to understand it, since it was I who, only a moment before, had somewhat awkwardly asked her, "I hope we'll meet again?" Her reply might have been, "Sure, whenever you're free," or at least an indefinite, "Anytime," but she only repeated, "We'll meet again," and to make matters worse added, "someday." It's true that she said it in a sweet tone of voice but that doesn't mean anything, because Victoria is essentially unable to be rude—well, except when she calls Dante Gabriel Rossetti a wretch.

It was thus made very clear to me that she was trying to avoid another date, and that she was happy to leave the possibility of our meeting again entirely to chance. This perhaps explains why I didn't reply, "Okay, why don't we meet tomorrow, if you want." I didn't, since it would have left her with no way out.

I'm sure that if we ever happened to meet again, we'd be able to have a drink or a cup of coffee together and reminisce about our walks in London, and frankly that's almost the worst thing, that she didn't even seem angry, hurt or offended. In other words, she didn't care enough about me to feel resentful and this makes it all the more painful; I've disappointed her, like many others before me, I suppose, and she just pities me.

It was partly due to bad luck that our burgeoning relationship ended, but essentially I'm the one to blame. Now that it's all over and I know I've lost her forever, I see all the more clearly how deeply in love with her I was, and that she must have felt something for me too; of this I'm sure. In retrospect I realize that I should have shown her more clearly how I felt, that I should have said, quite simply, "I think I'm in love with you, Victoria." She would have said something in response, I don't know what, to show that she also cared for me. Maybe she would have said something like, "I also have feelings for you," with that expression women often use when they want to let us know they're not completely indifferent toward us; and then we would have gone on to talk about seeing each other again, and the landscape I now behold, a sky aching under the weight of black clouds, spat at by the gray sea, wouldn't have the power to upset me, because we would already have arranged to meet again somewhere, probably in San Sebastián, to have dinner together at the Urepel, a restaurant overlooking the Urumea River.

Now, after all that has happened, it's easy to say with hindsight that anything would have been better than what I actually did. But at the time I was so scared of disappointing her by saying or doing the wrong thing that I felt the need for a tried-and-tested formula to win her affection. What I needed was something more convincing and above all more original than, "I think I'm in love with you."

Actually, I was tempted more than once, while we walked around London, to interrupt her and tell her just that, but I was afraid that such a remark would end it all, would even offend her by revealing how I had misjudged her friendliness toward me. This tendency of us men to want to go beyond the mere platonic friendship women are often satisfied with is something they find particularly annoying; they feel betrayed when they find out how badly we misinterpret their friendly affection, and all too often this brings an end to the very friendship we want to transcend.

This was why I decided against openly showing her my feelings. I didn't want to put our fledgling, fragile relationship at risk. However, I see clearly now that the worst thing she could have done had I told her something like, "I think I'm in love with you," would be to laugh it off and say, "Come on, it's only your imagination," or, "You don't even know me," or even something more philosophical, such as, "You don't really love me, you just want to love me."

Any decision would have been better than the one I ended up making. It's all so clear now in view of the way things turned out. Nevertheless, without wishing to sound entirely blameless, I want to say that I had my reasons for doing what I did. I thought it would be more convenient for me to write to her rather than tell her what I wanted to say, since, for anyone with any literary skills whatsoever, it's easier to convey such things in writing.

Firstly because it helps you avoid a face-to-face encounter, but more importantly because it lets you hide your true intentions behind a literary façade, so that if things don't go as planned you can always say it was only words, mere fiction. This is why I believe writers, with some noble exceptions, are usually cowards.

But in this case, trying to win over Victoria through writing seemed all the more justified, because a couple of years previously, in similar circumstances, it had proved extremely successful with Eugenia. At the time, at least, I wouldn't have thought it excessive to use the word "successful" to describe the effect my note had on her, and it was natural to expect that what had worked with Eugenia would also work with Victoria, for they were alike in so many ways: apart from belonging to the same social class, they were both intelligent, educated women with an interest in literature.

The main problem, however, was that I had almost completely forgotten the words I had used in my note to Eugenia, and that, precisely because I had forgotten them, I became obsessed with the note, or rather with the idea of sending Victoria the exact same note. A similar one wouldn't have done. I had gotten it firmly into my mind that it had to be the same text, word for word, so I tried everything to get it back. That's more or less what happened, to put it briefly.

I suppose that to some extent this happens to everybody: you forget something that usually trips off your tongue, then become obsessed with calling it to mind. I for one have often found myself in this situation, especially since I started to use the computer to write, because, being a late arrival to the world of information technology, I easily lose parts of my documents in the inevitable

process of cutting and pasting. And usually on such occasions, whatever I've deleted—a simple line, a word, even
the heading of a note—suddenly seems irreplaceable, as
though it had been the result of a unique moment of
inspiration.

In such situations I feel convinced that only the
words that I've lost and the exact way they were strung
together can adequately express my thoughts, and that if
I don't remember them I won't be able to say or write a
single word. Thus I become obsessed with retrieving them
and can spend hours and days on end at the computer,
wasting my time, calling all my computer-literate friends
for help, because I'm incapable of recalling exactly the
line, paragraph or fragment I've lost. And it has to be the
same text, word for word.

Of course, in the case of the note I'd written to Eugenia and wanted to use again with Victoria, a certain nostalgia for the lost word seems more understandable. For
one thing, as I said before, I well remembered the effect
the note had had on Eugenia, for it had suddenly filled
her with a fiery passion for me, and this naturally made
me all the more eager to recover it. Moreover, because I'd
written the note by hand, I couldn't even entertain my
obsession by frantically searching my hard disk for it,
which made things even worse.

Sedano, a psychoanalyst by profession and a friend
and colleague of sorts, describes me as an "obsessive neurotic." According to him, this isn't a condition one is born
with (I myself prefer to call it a condition rather than an
illness), but one that usually develops early in life. Though
he's probably right, I don't think that as a child I resembled such lascivious children as, for example, Freud's Rat
Man, who got erections at the tender age of four. How-

ever, what I can assure you, for I do have extensive knowledge in this area, is that obsessive neurosis is certainly not a psychological trait that improves with age.

In the carefree days of youth you share your ideas and plans with others without giving it a second thought. You don't feel the need to selfishly keep every idea to yourself as if it were patent-pending, probably because you're more prolific, as well as more self-confident, in the sense that when you lose a good idea you feel you can easily come up with a better one. In fact you feel like an inexhaustible source of ideas. Poems seem almost to gush from your mind—or your heart, for I'm not sure where poems are generated. Enough, in any case, to enable you to send love letters to all the girls you fall for. Moreover, when we're young we're also less inhibited about copying from poetry anthologies: we have an anything-goes attitude.

Anyway, what's certainly true is that when I was young I wouldn't have become so obsessed with a lost text, because I could write a new one just like that, or fall back on a line that I particularly liked. "I opened a window to the sea" was an opening line I frequently used. I certainly wouldn't have lost any sleep over it, and this is precisely the attitude Rossetti himself should have taken, but the poor wretch got it into his mind that his poems were terribly sublime, and became obsessed with recovering them. Something similar happened to me.

It was something that Victoria couldn't understand: the selfishness of a creative mind, its vanity. "People like that would rather see an entire Gothic cathedral demolished than one line of their work erased," I remember her saying. Her voice, usually so sweet, became tense whenever she repeated what a wretch Rossetti was. And she never seemed to be joking; in fact, whenever she brought the matter up she looked very serious, deadly serious.

I haven't always been like this. My literary work—if it can be so called, for apart from some commissioned work, I've only published one novel, *Farewell, Sadness*, an early work whose title reflects the mood in which I wrote it— my literary production, I say, has never really obsessed me. I mean that I'm not one of those people who go around brooding on the brilliance of their silly ideas and writing them down on scraps of paper. In fact, the day I lost the manuscript that has just been returned to me (not some lines or a paragraph, but a whole novel which I suppose I considered valuable at the time), I didn't take it too seriously, and certainly didn't become obsessed with it. I simply decided that I'd have to start writing a new one. And that meant writing a completely new one, because trying to reproduce the same text seemed too tedious. I have to admit, however, that for one reason or another I haven't yet been able to complete the task.

I'm not even sure how I managed to lose it, though I'm certain it was in a hotel room in Paris. I remember I was with a German girl who didn't shave her legs because her boyfriend wouldn't let her. Her hairy legs gave me a feeling I find difficult to describe. It was disturbing because since the hairiness of her legs was in direct contrast to the sheer whiteness of the sheets, it constantly reminded me of her boyfriend who, she said, was a tough Bavarian biker, and I'm not ashamed to say that the touch of those long, soft hairs became somewhat worrying in the darkness.

After we had had rather disappointing sex a couple of times, I told her that the Condor Legion had bombed Gernika, and explained what this event had meant to the

Basque people. I didn't say it on purpose, as a sort of revenge for the fact that the sex hadn't been great, but rather to somehow point out the Basque Country on the map, because earlier on she had asked me where I came from. "You too, then," was her dejected response, more dejected than I could have imagined, as if I were blaming her for the bombs.

"Only yesterday I was having dinner with a Polish guy and he told me the same thing: that we Germans had bombed their country," she said, though she couldn't remember the name of the city. At first, she only said they had had dinner together, but I was sure she had also slept with him. "Gernika, though, was a sacred town for us Basques," was my reply, in an attempt to set myself apart from the Pole, though I was sure she didn't know what a sacred town meant. I considered how to explain it in case she asked: the tree, the gatherings around the tree, the oldest democracy in Europe... but in the end she didn't ask. After a long pause, she got out of bed and declared that she didn't think she would ever have the luck to sleep with someone who hadn't been wronged by her countrymen.

I also got up. We got dressed with our backs to each other. I knew I wouldn't see her again, and thought I ought to make some kind of statement. The folder containing the manuscript of my novel was lying on the chest of drawers; I wouldn't see it for a long time, but I didn't know that then, of course. I picked it up and told her, "It's all in here," the way I used to do when I couldn't think of anything else to say.

Thinking back, perhaps that's why, before the advent of photocopy machines, I had the habit of carrying the manuscript of the novel around with me when I traveled.

It allowed me to boast to foreigners, usually girls, of being a novelist, and an all the more interesting one for writing in a strange language, something that also had the advantage of allowing me to avoid any true assessment of my work. Then again, I might also have been in that revision stage which some writers (unfortunately not all) tend to delay, not only because of perfectionism, but more so because they are afraid of publishing their work and leaving it at the mercy of the reader's critical judgment. Perhaps some part of me even wanted to lose it, precisely to protect it from being published. This is similar to what many mothers do to their children: in an effort to protect them from the dangers of the outside world, they end up spoiling them.

Of course all this is speculation, as Sedano likes to call it. I have almost inadvertently become aware that the real reason I lost the novel may have been that secretly I found it poor. This is something that's very difficult for a novelist to admit, unless he finds himself at a real low with no one to turn to, in that pitiful state in which one keeps on writing novels knowing full well they're bad. And clearly this wasn't my case. Anyway, I confess that whatever the reasons for losing it, if we can speak about reasons at all, I certainly did everything in my power to get it back. As soon as I noticed I had lost it, I phoned the hotel, and the next time I was in Paris went there to ask about it in person.

It was a *Frantour* hotel, one of the best, close to the Hilton and in a quiet area near the Eiffel Tower. My enquiry didn't seem to surprise them much. I mean the fact that it was a manuscript I'd lost, rather than a lighter or a comb, say, caused no particular impression, as if it were quite natural for writers to leave their novels in hotel rooms, whether consciously or unconsciously. Indeed, I got the sense that they didn't take great pains to find it, apart from the odd phone call by the receptionist that finally came to nothing.

I was bold enough to ask them if they had looked everywhere, for I could hardly believe it could simply disappear into thin air. In theory it should have been easy to find: no one could read it and it had no objective value, unlike a gold lighter, in which case, it would have been pointless to go back for it. A manuscript isn't something you throw away like a used toothbrush. The written word is usually treated with respect, and everybody knows that, for the writer at least, it can be of incalculable value. Moreover, it doesn't take up much space, and neither stains nor smells.

But the fact is that I had lost it, and there was no trace of it anywhere. All I could do was leave my name and address and ask them to send it to me if ever they came across it.

I never forgot that loss, or the contents of the novel, at least not completely. The novel never left my mind; I have subconsciously retained many of its images and passages and used them many times since then. After all, we don't get all that many ideas throughout our lives, and we usually repeat two or three images and the odd metaphor now and again. Each time I write, "The sea of slate," for instance, it feels like I'm doing it for the first time, and I have reused many of the events in the lost novel without noticing it.

Though it never entirely escaped my mind, I ended up with only a vague idea of its plot, and curiously enough—what a funny thing memory is—I completely forgot passages that I can now recall merely by glancing at the manuscript's folder. In any case, what amazes me most is that the loss didn't affect me all that much. I must have been in mourning for the lost novel for some time, but then I succeeded in setting my mind on other things. This is something that, unfortunately, I'm unable to do these days, for as I said before, though I only needed three words to tell Victoria I was in love with her (women only need to hear the words "I love you," if they are spoken with sincerity), I'm ashamed to admit that I was obsessed by the idea of retrieving the words I had sent to Eugenia, to my own disgrace.

I first met Eugenia in Aranjuez. The Ministry of Culture had summoned me to a meeting in Madrid to organize a poetry anthology of the work of poets of the four languages of Spain—that's what it was called, *Poetas de las cuatro lenguas*. I met Sedano on the way and we took the opportunity to go to Aranjuez, since neither of us had been there before.

We had been walking for a long time and, feeling tired, decided to relax in a café beside the theater. All the tables were taken, but Sedano caught sight of a female colleague sitting at a table with another woman, and walked over to ask if we could sit with them.

Sedano introduced his friend to me, and she in turn introduced Eugenia to us. I forgot her name immediately, because I usually get very nervous when I'm introduced to somebody. My mind flits over a thousand things; above all, I worry about my clammy hands. As soon as we sat down, Eugenia (whose name, as I said, I didn't know yet), without specifically addressing either of us, said, "*O sea que Vascos*," "So you're Basque, then."

I said yes. Sedano kept quiet and his friend hastily added, "But civilized, eh? At least this one," pinching him on the chin. "He's an angel."

Eugenia stared at me, waiting for me to say something, and, pressed by her look, I had to admit that I was also a civilized Basque. After this declaration on my part, Sedano and Eugenia's friend started talking about their acquaintances, or rather, dismantling their personalities.

The woman was quite nasty. She diagnosed every person she mentioned. She called somebody hysterical. I remember it well, because it was the fist time I heard about Flora the Cat: "She gets pleasure but she's never satisfied. She's like Flora the Cat: she screams when she's being fucked and cries when she's not."

"You're so bad," Eugenia told her, and just to say something I told her that Sedano was also a bit evil-minded, and that probably all psychiatrists were. After that we stayed silent while the other two talked. Sedano said that Felix Guattari's work was essential to understanding "the quantum void." He seemed to do so without embarrassment, though he had more than once admitted to me, after a night out and a few too many, that he didn't understand a single word of Deleuze and Guattari. The woman for her part repeated the term "*jouissance*" over and over, though she had serious trouble pronouncing it right.

"I'm glad," Eugenia said.

She caught me unawares, and apparently noticed the confused look on my face.

"That you're a civilized Basque."

And she fell silent again. I'm not the kind of person who travels the world pretending to be an authentic Basque, but sometimes it's hard to know how deeply you have to repress your identity to please others. Since being Basque is sometimes associated with terrible things, I tend to repress even the most insignificant aspect that might be tied in with the Basque stereotype in order to avoid offending other people. And because it makes things easier, I suppose. But this tendency of mine frustrates me, so I decided to avoid "the Basque issue" at all costs.

To change the subject, I told her that her lips were like strawberries. It was true, they looked like strawberries drizzled with lemon juice: glossy.

"That's why I'm in Aranjuez," she replied, not seriously, but not joking either; with a somewhat weary air.

I don't know why I didn't keep that silly remark to myself. Perhaps because of the overwhelming presence of strawberries in that place. They were everywhere: on the street stalls, on the tables in the café. I told her that in Aranjuez everything took on the color of strawberries: "*On voit la vie en fraise.*"

She laughed.

"It must be an unavoidable metaphor for a poet."

Her laughter attracted Sedano's attention; he interrupted what he was saying to his psychiatrist friend about Deleuze to warn Eugenia.

"Be careful with him, he's a real Casanova."

Eugenia replied that Casanova himself, Giovanni Giacomo, had been in Aranjuez in 1767 to attend the opening of the theater, and that since then the male talent for seduction appeared to have gone steadily downhill. Her friend, attempting to play down this remark, put in that Eugenia knew a great deal about the history and art of Madrid.

"Eugenia. Beautiful name," I said, adding that it reminded me of the Victoria Eugenia Theater in San Sebastián, of the romantic area with the golden color of sandstone in twilight, and the tawny reflection of the bridge lights on the river.

She admitted that San Sebastián is beautiful. Her voice seemed to grow wearier, but I ignored this and told her that her name also reminded me of Eugénie les Bains.

I could have mentioned Eugenia de Montijo, but the French health spa is what I thought of first.

"Thank you. Eugénie is a good place to eat."

"Do you know it?"

"Sure."

Not knowing what to say, I fell silent again. When I'm with people I don't know, my excessive desire to please them prevents me from acting naturally. In an attempt to sound original I try to avoid everyday topics like the weather and politics, and either find myself in a total mental block or get lost in pointless and boring digressions. According to Sedano, being a bore is one of the characteristics of the neurotic: "Obsessive neurotics like you are so concerned with sounding extraordinary that you end up being tedious." It's true that Sedano links everything I tell him about myself to my condition, but sadly, he's probably right. As he says, "In the moment of their encounter with the Other, obsessive neurotics fail."

This is precisely what I fancied the three of them were thinking. In any case, all three were looking at me as if waiting for me to say something, and feeling compelled to go on talking, I started to tell them about the couple of occasions when I had the opportunity to eat at Eugénie, and how the waitresses serve the covered dishes: after reciting the dish's long list of ingredients while holding the lids by the handles (*filet de turbot au beurre de persil et fruits du mendiant avec* this and that), when they finally lift the lids over the diners' heads, like cymbal players in an orchestra, a terrible stink emerges from their armpits and spreads across the table.

Nobody said anything, probably because they found the anecdote unpleasant. So we remained silent for a while, until Sedano and his friend resumed their conversation about Deleuze, and Eugenia asked me about my job.

"Wait!" she said, reaching out and putting her hand over my mouth, "I bet you I can guess!"

She slumped back in her seat with half-closed eyes, as if she were about to draw a portrait of me.

"I know. You're a journalist!" she said.

It seemed to me that she had intended this as an insult. Nevertheless, I told her that I considered myself more of a writer than a journalist.

"The ability to write is the greatest gift on earth," she said suddenly, apparently in earnest. She talked about writers she liked. I remember she mentioned Delibes, whose style she admired. She started to quote one of his lines from memory and then left it in the air, unfinished, feigning a swoon to indicate the overpowering pleasure it gave her. After this display, she said she thought him extremely good. Actually, her exact words were, "He's a great fucking writer."

She was an attorney, and though her Spanish was very formal, even to the point of ostentation, she spontaneously inserted some swearwords and common expressions here and there. She asked me many questions about what I was writing and reading. I tried to avoid them, and to say something intelligent about the authors she mentioned, though they weren't among my favorites. I also told her about the poets of the four languages, thinking it would impress her, and of course I told her what the Basque poet Aresti had said: "Only he is Spanish who knows all the four tongues of Spain." I think she liked it. Most probably, she was surprised that I had called Basque a Spanish language, but she didn't say anything. I nevertheless noticed how, for a moment, she considered whether she had misjudged me. To make sure, she asked me if I liked Madrid.

I told her the truth, that I hardly knew it, though I had been there many times. I told her that in the past, Basque people only came to Madrid when they had some duty to fulfill, and that they tried to make their stay as brief as possible. In fact, people would boast about having done the round trip the quickest. We hated Madrid because we had to go there on account of all the absurd paperwork that had to be dealt with in the various government offices, and it's hard to find a place beautiful when you're forced to go there. We used to associate Madrid with the Franco years: most of the men we saw in the streets and bars, with their suits, sunglasses and thin moustaches, looked like undercover cops to us.

More recently, after having gained political autonomy, we've become aware that administrative incompetence and arrogance are not the exclusive patrimony of the Spanish capital.

She replied, with a grave look, that Madrid was a very beautiful city and that I wasn't being fair to it. Or to its inhabitants, she added after a short pause.

I didn't object, since to some extent I agreed with her. Moreover, I told her that, come to think about it, Madrid was probably one of the most beautiful capitals in Europe and that I intended to go there as a tourist sometime, with no special purpose, as though I were visiting Rome, Paris or London, and that I'd get to know it well. After all, I told her, that was the problem, I didn't really know it.

No doubt this delighted her. It's understandable. We all get emotional when someone praises our hometown. She asked me to give her a call when I came to visit, and said she would show me around.

"I'll be your guide."

After rummaging in her bag, she took out a card and gave it to me. Then she glanced at her watch and said it was getting late for her. She repeated her invitation to show me around Madrid whenever I had some spare time, and the four of us rose from the table. Then we accompanied them to the theater, where they had parked their car.

I called her a couple of weeks later. She couldn't remember my name, so I had to tell her I was the guy she had met in Aranjuez, which was of course utterly humiliating. "Oh sure! The writer!" was her reply. She said she was glad I'd decided to call. It was obvious, however, that my call was ill timed. In the end she told me she was very busy and had to go, but we arranged to meet the following day.

We were to meet at her workplace, a law firm on Ortega y Gasset Street. While I was waiting in the reception area I saw several men coming and going: men in their forties with beards, ties and tweed jackets. Looking at them I had the impression that the firm was staffed by the kind of left-wing people who turn from labor law to administrative law as they gain more power in the institutions. The delicate carpets were oriental, probably Persian. The furniture was classical, to the taste of the new ruling class, and most likely English. When they showed me into Eugenia's office, I found her sitting at a table with green leather upholstery, her arms folded.

She unfolded them, and for a moment I thought she was going to say something like, "Everything under this ceiling belongs to me," but she only started massaging her temples and wearily complained about having too much work and too little energy. "I'm so tired and I've got so much work to do!"

Of course I felt obliged to tell her I would leave and come again some other day, but she stretched out her arm as though ordering me to stop, though I hadn't stirred. "It's not that." She told me she was overloaded with work and, making a visible effort to cheer up, added that she was nevertheless very happy to see me.

The room gave onto a spacious balcony overlooking Ortega y Gasset Street. On the other side of the road I could see one of the few nineteenth-century palaces that are still standing: classical in structure but with understated modernist adornments. I told her the view was spectacular. Flattered, as if I had told her she had nice legs, she drew back the curtains completely and opened the window, letting in a roar of traffic.

"Do you know what I like most about Madrid?"

Though she was blinking up at the sun, I was unable to think of an answer.

"The sky," she said. "The brightness. I would yearn for that if I lived in the north."

I gave in. The sky was clearly brighter than ours: a brilliant pale blue.

When I lowered my eyes I caught her looking at her watch. I was about to tell her that if she was that pressed for time she should have told me when I called her, but didn't dare. I don't know why it occurred to me to remark on how many trees there were in Madrid. I had become aware of this in my last trips.

"It's full of beautiful trees, yes." She turned from the balcony and suddenly perked up. "The fact is that you don't want to see the beauty of this city," she said, and without letting me contradict her, added: "It has more green areas than any other European capital." She pointed at the street. "It has more than half a million trees, but you prefer to think it's the desert."

At last I was able to speak. I agreed that Madrid was full of beautiful trees, while San Sebastián (I added, thinking it would please her) looked more like Medina del Campo every year. That's what an aunt of mine says. She's never been to Medina del Campo, but she imagines it's barren.

"Oh no! San Sebastián is beautiful!" she objected. But she was evidently pleased that I had criticized it. Her face softened.

I said it wasn't as elegant as it used to be. But of course it still possessed some valuable remnants of its more stylish past. I was about to add that it increasingly resembled any other Spanish city; the street furniture, for example, was chosen from the same catalogs they used in Madrid or Chiclana. But though I truly believed this, I felt that saying it would have been like betraying my own country.

On the bookcase, a clock struck. It had several golden spheres that hit one another and left a thin metallic sound trailing into the air. We both stood looking at it until the echo of the carillon was lost. Then I told her I didn't want to bother her any more, and that I would go to the Reina Sofía museum for a walk. But she raised her open hand again, in that gesture of hers—not exactly commanding, but somewhat imposing—and told me to wait, that if I gave her another half an hour she would show me something I almost certainly hadn't seen.

Without waiting for an answer she picked up the phone and asked for her car. I wouldn't say she did it to show off, but she seemed completely aware of what she was doing.

It was a small car, which she drove leaning forward, her nose nearly touching the steering wheel, but with great energy and care, as many women do. We only covered a small distance; she took me to the nearby Royal Botanical Gardens.

We walked among plants and trees and long lines of schoolchildren. The place is truly an oasis, sheltered from the deafening traffic of the Paseo del Prado.

I had to admit that it was the first time I saw many of the plants whose fruits I have often eaten. In fact, some of them, such as artichokes, so ordinary on a plate, looked lush and exotic. I'm not sure why, but it seemed like it wasn't the first time she had shown someone around the gardens. Although I would have preferred to go on looking at all the culinary plants I didn't know, she led me down a fixed route, like those professional guides who won't let anybody leave the tour. I remember she talked a lot, on this as on later occasions, about Charles III of Spain, the man who had created the Botanical Gardens. She believed that the Spanish Enlightenment had been brushed over to the point of making us believe it never existed, and she thanked God that the *madrileños* had been able to recover some of their self-esteem with Tierno Galvan.

When we came out of the Botanical Gardens I asked her if she wanted to have tapas. She said no, adding that we Basques were always thinking about eating and drinking. I assumed, since she kept her car keys in her hand, that she intended to go back to her office, and trying to beat her to it said, "You'll have to go back, of course." She must have noticed my helplessness, though, because although she answered in the affirmative—"I'd have to leave, yes,"—she didn't leave straight away. She asked me if she could read some of my writing, just to say something I guess, and I answered that reading anything of mine when she had thousands of classics at her disposal would be a waste of time. She stayed silent for a long time, then exclaimed, "How wonderful to be able to write, to be able to express your feelings in words," and I had the impression that she was being completely honest.

Then she told me pensively how lucky I was, and finally cried out, "Well, I'm off." I had already told her I would stay. She started to walk away, then turned and said, "Call me some time—we'll have lunch," and continued toward Moyano Hill.

I didn't call her until a month later, when I had the oppor-tunity to go to a conference in Madrid on the state of Spanish literature. Since by that time bringing in some form of representation of the literatures of the periphery had become a formal obligation in events of this kind, the Basque Writers' Association had been invited, and I was chosen by lot to take part. I was about to call her from San Sebastián to let her know about my trip and invite her to the conference, because I thought the presence of all those well-known writers might give me some standing in her eyes. But in the end I decided against calling her, because she would have become aware that my participation in the conference was at best purely symbolic.

Conferences, talks and meetings generally leave me depressed, since my performance is usually much poorer than I'd like. That was certainly the case this time. I was terribly uncomfortable among the "top-ten" literati, and even felt ashamed when I was introduced as the author of *Landscape and Gastronomy*. At lunch, I couldn't think of a thing to say to anyone, so I escaped after just a quick cof-fee, saying I had to catch a plane.

It was from that same place, the Ateneo, that I called her for the first time. I really can't explain why; I wasn't particularly eager to see her. I suppose I was driven by curiosity, by a desire to see how our new relationship might evolve. The person I spoke to in her office told me she had gone out for lunch. When I finally got hold of her after three or four attempts, she didn't sound very happy to hear from me. Nevertheless, I found her voice very sensual, and found myself imagining her fleshy lips.

"We can meet in the evening," she said—not very willingly, I thought. When I asked her what time she was thinking of, she said six o'clock. So as usual I went to the Reina Sofia Museum to look at Chillida's sculptures, because they make me feel at home.

We arranged to meet at the Westin Palace Hotel. We were sitting under the glass dome when she started talking about the building. In fact, she always told me something about the places she took me to: the style of the building, the architect's name, things like that. I can't recall what she told me on that occasion, but I remember feeling I had disappointed her because I hadn't stayed right there, at the Palace Hotel.

When she asked me what I wanted to do, I told her I didn't know. Whatever she wanted: anything. Apparently that disappointed her too. "Anything, anything. Tell me what you really want," she told me impatiently. It was true that I really didn't care one way or the other. I didn't feel like doing anything special. Moreover, I didn't know, even approximately, how much time we had, or to be more precise, whether we were going to have dinner together. Nor did I want to ask. I didn't want to give her the chance to say that Basques are always thinking about food.

On the other hand, I didn't much like the atmosphere under the dome. It was full of men in blue blazers, their hair combed back with shiny hair gel. Not to mention the women with poodles on their laps. An improvised television studio had been built just in front of us, where a TV star was interviewing an old man I didn't recognize. Not only that: among a group of men standing behind the TV crew, I caught sight of Martinez de Leunda, an EAJ party

representative who lives around the corner from me.* He
also saw me, and I'm sure that, as our eyes met, he asked
himself what I was doing at the Palace Hotel, or what I
was up to with Eugenia, or maybe both.

Suddenly she said, "What's wrong with you Basques?"
She would ask this question very often, and not
knowing what to answer, I would avoid the issue as much
as possible with comments like, "It's a complicated issue,"
or, "I don't understand it myself." That's also what I told
her this time, that it was a complicated issue. I didn't feel
like talking politics, and I was hungry because I hadn't
eaten lunch at the conference. Besides, I wasn't lying to
her, for the issue is indeed difficult. "It's not something
you can just explain in a couple of sentences," I added
and, trying to change the subject, suggested we take a
walk, not daring to mention the possibility of going out
for dinner.

She got up without a word and we went outside.
"Honestly, I don't know what's happening to us," I said,
trying to restore normality, even though I wasn't sure there
was anything wrong with me. She answered, "It's as complicated as understanding that you can't go around putting bullets in people's heads." Of course I could have told
her that I don't go around shooting anybody, and that furthermore I think it's a terrible thing to do, but I chose to
remain silent. She drove her small car very carefully
through the busy traffic, energetically gripping the steering wheel. Meanwhile I had time to think about the
absurdity of the situation. It was absurd because it was
clear that if she agreed to take a walk with me from time

---

* The EAJ is a conservative, nationalist political party in the Basque
Country. (T.N.)

to time, it was only because she felt obliged to do so out of love for Madrid, and because she had told me in Aranjuez that she would. Besides, I wasn't sure why I had called her; I only knew that I was curious to see where things might go if I pushed them along a bit.

She finally left the car in the parking lot by the Callao Cinema, and we walked up Santo Domingo Hill to the Royal Palace.

We stayed there for a while. It was a pleasant place, sheltered from the noise of the street. We could see the silent white and red lines of the car lights at the other end of Campo del Moro. The sky was an intense blue. Luckily we were out of visiting hours. Nevertheless, Eugenia talked about the Bourbons for a long time, about Sabatini's staircase and Gasparini's living room (or is it the other way around?) and about the room of mirrors. She knew everything about the Royal Palace. It suddenly occurred to her that the carriage museum might still be open, but fortunately it was also closed. Next we crossed to the Plaza de Oriente and walked on up the hill. I suggested that we take a walk in the area around the opera house, because it's one of my favorite places in Madrid. But she glanced at her watch and told me she still had some things to do at her office. We therefore headed back toward the parking lot, while we talked about our tastes in literature, though to tell the truth she did most of the talking. It was obvious that she was a faithful reader of *Babelia*, the literary supplement of *El País*. She mentioned it twice, and it amazed her to hear that I didn't know many of the books she considered extraordinary—"a must," in her words. So I ended up saying I knew some of them, at the risk of being caught in a lie. However, she didn't seem to care much about my opinion, and I didn't have much trouble deceiving her, since she didn't question me about them. However, she kept telling me how lucky I was to have the ability to write, and that she'd like to read something I'd written. And that was how she took leave of me on this occasion too: "I hope I'll be able to read some of your writing soon."

Every time we met, she did the same thing. We would arrange to meet at her office or in some well-known place—I remember having met her at Hardy and at Gijon, as well as the Palace Hotel—and then take a small tour which was meant to be original. On one occasion she took me to the Tower of Spain. On the top floor are the headquarters of a regional house, the House of Asturias, I think, where, for an admission fee, you can go out onto the balcony. And it is indeed a breathtaking sight. Another time, we walked around the Golden Age quarter where Zerain, the Basque cider maker, is based, and where all the writers of the Spanish Golden Age, Lope de Vega, Góngora, Quevedo and Cervantes, among others, lived within an area of a few square meters. She told me something about each of them: when and where they were born and died, the titles of their most famous works, some quotes... the kind of thing learned people like to say. We walked around La Trinidad convent for a long time, because Cervantes, whose daughter was the abbess of the convent, is said to be buried there, though it's not known in which grave. The Academy of the Spanish Language organizes a mass on April 23 every year, which Eugenia always attends; at least that's what she told me. Not really for the service, but because it's a unique opportunity to see all the major writers. "The Parnassus, you know?" she used to tell me with sparkling eyes.

"How lucky to be able to write!" she would exclaim dreamily.

She always used expressions like, "The ability to put one's feelings into words," or, "The art of words." One day I told her that writers normally had to fight against words; that words were our enemies. I don't know why I said it. She found it very interesting, though, and asked me to elaborate. I couldn't think of anything to say; to tell the truth, these are simple paradoxes, and I don't like them much. So to dodge the issue I told her that I'd explain it to her in writing, and she told me she'd appreciate it, her eyes sparkling again; she'd look forward to it. Then, as usual, she looked at her watch and took her leave.

She'd suddenly cry, "How late it is!" and we'd say goodbye. This generally happened between six and seven. She would leave by car, and I would stay wherever we happened to be. She never told me directly that she had a husband and children. She mentioned them indirectly, evasively, and I never knew how many she had—children, I mean—but it must have been more than one, for I remember she used the plural.

I found this kind of secrecy exciting. As for her body, it was her mouth that I found most attractive. As I've said, her lips were sensual: the upper lip was thick—fleshy is the word I have used, and I can't find a more appropriate one. They always looked moist and fresh. Whenever we met and parted, we used to kiss each other on both cheeks, or rather, slightly touch one another's cheeks as a matter of courtesy. Once, however, I missed her cheek (I never know which side to go for first), and in the muddle I felt the freshness of her lips, and the unexpected kiss I got on that occasion thrilled me more than all the ardent ones I would later receive from her. Besides, she also knew how to enhance the attractiveness of her mouth. When she wanted to emphasize something she was saying, she would leave the last word hanging in the air, as if suspended from her lips, which she kept half open. She would close her eyes slightly, too, which made her look like she was about to start panting.

Her way of speaking was also very sensual. When we spoke on the phone, there was the hint of a veiled meaning in every trivial remark she made, especially when she said, "Write something for me one of these days, will you?" But at the same time she knew how to be firm, even hard, and there was nothing you could do when she glanced at her watch and decided it was time for her to go. She didn't really show her intentions, her desires, and though this naturally made me somewhat uncomfortable, it also made her more appealing.

I used to call her quite often from San Sebastián just to hear her voice, and it was always the same. She recommended books to me, based, I assume, on the reviews in *El País*. I think she used to learn parts of the reviews by heart—she had a very good memory—and recite them to me as if they were her own words. Then she would ask me how things were in the Basque Country, what the hell was happening to us, why everyone there had gone crazy, and so on. And she always concluded by asking me when she would be able to read some of my work.

Until one day I decided to write her a note and leave all that ambiguity behind. I say a note, because I wrote it on a thick white invitation card. This kind of paper is elegant and well suited to a short text. I wrote it without giving it much thought; I mean it didn't give me too much trouble. "I'll knock on the door and you'll be lying on the bed, naked." It was an ordinary scene in a hotel room. She would be lying on silk sheets and I would appear with a bottle of champagne in my hand and a couple of glasses in my pockets. Like in the film *Sabrina*. Naturally, I mentioned the cold pearls of water on the bottle which would soothe the fire in her thighs, followed by all the other clichés: flowers, silk, the smoothness of her skin, the secret scents... and toward the end, having lingered on a couple of metaphors, I left allegories aside and explicitly mentioned her ass, my desire to see it, to touch it, so I could apprehend reality, know she was real. "You were merely a dream, which has now become flesh and blood as I behold your naked body," and in the same line, "I want to be sated by you, to drink from your mouth..." I don't think there's any need to go on, especially considering that this isn't by any means a memory of which I'm proud.

I don't know how I managed to behave so boldly, though it's true that it's easier to say things like this in writing. Most probably I was hiding behind my literary pursuit. After all, that's precisely the function of literature: to offer a shelter for things we otherwise cannot say. Literature liberates. The writer's—and, more importantly, the reader's—literary pursuit can transform anything, even what we would ordinarily call obscene, into something beautiful. I know this may be reminiscent of the hypocritical distinction people make between erotica and pornography, but I really think that's how it works.

I'm not sure I gave it this much thought when I was writing the note. Probably not. I knew it intuitively. I knew that even if she took what I had written the wrong way (after all, she was a married woman and the mention of her buttocks was not the lewdest one in the note), she couldn't blame me, partly thanks to the privilege of literary expression, but most importantly because she was the one who had repeatedly said she wanted to see my writing.

If writing the note was relatively easy, making the decision to send it was more difficult, even though I knew that normally women are not put off by a straightforward manner. In fact I'd say they generally prefer forthright propositions, at least when they're made with a minimum of style, to the silly roundabout paths we men often feel obliged to take. This is certainly true when they're in a receptive mood, and even when they're not, they're usually polite. I mean that they seldom disapprove of a well-mannered proposition, because it flatters them, and in any case one can be sure that they won't shout it from the rooftops, as men often do. Women are loyal.

But theory is one thing, practice quite another. Our personal histories influence us enormously. Women who now make jokes about their husbands' poor sexual performance tried, in their better days, to make us believe they didn't care about sex. They accepted sexual relationships only because, at best, they fitted into the customary cinema-dancing-tea scheme, and because they felt obliged to give in to the boys' insistent demands.

French girls, however, were different: they were said to like kissing. Not a bit like the locals! And I include in the latter group a kind of girlfriend I had in Bayonne, who caressed me sadly, with well-intentioned resignation.

How misinformed we must have been, that even with French girls we felt compelled to keep a period of abstinence—though no longer than four days. This I knew from experience, because I once dated a girl from Condom, a French town close to the Basque Country, and though the name of her hometown gave me the opportunity to raise the matter from the beginning, I went to Mount Igeldo to have tea with her on three successive days without even touching her. On the fourth day, however, she told me she couldn't go out because her family wouldn't let her. And I stayed at home, bereft and heartbroken, as one does at such times. I was staring out of the window at the empty streets, probably with a poem in my mind ("I am sitting at the window, alone, looking out over the lonely streets"), when suddenly I saw the girl from Condom on the opposite balcony in the arms of a vacationer from Madrid who constantly organized parties.

Until the day I wrote the note, I had seen Eugenia only five or six times, including the afternoon we had met in Aranjuez, and we had never talked about our "relationship." Furthermore, I had no particular reason to think she might be interested in me; at most she was curious about my writing, which I thought might merely be down to good manners, or pure hypocrisy, something people believe they ought to ask when they meet a writer. There were also the trips she took me on, but again I had the impression that she didn't play Cicero's role very willingly, but rather out of a sense of duty. After all, this happens to many of us, especially those of us who live in cities we can show off. I've often regretted having thoughtlessly told people to call me whenever they happened to be in San Sebastián.

These thoughts occupied me for some days, and I kept postponing my decision to send the note. Procrastination is a symptom of obsessive neurosis. At least that's what Sedano says, and he's probably right. In any case, it was about a week after having written the note that I put it in the mailbox.

My decision to send it was prompted by the fact that I hadn't been able to talk to Eugenia for the past few days. Whenever I called her office they told me she was busy. Every day, morning and afternoon, I got the same answer, and naturally I came to imagine the worst, which in turn increased my desire to break the impasse we had reached. So finally one morning, having called her office yet again with no success, I put the note in an envelope and went to the post office, determined, as they say, to leave the final decision in the hands of fate. I held the envelope with its center (which I had previously marked) on the edge of the mailbox mouth: half in, half out. The idea was to hold the envelope horizontally on the very edge and, trying to kid myself as little as possible, let it go. If it fell outside I would break it off immediately; if it fell inside, I would let things take their course. It fell inside.

The period of expectancy didn't last long; I received a reply three days later. She called me in the morning, and immediately I knew the note had had a positive effect. When I picked up the phone I heard the most sensual sound I had ever heard in my life. I can testify that velvet voices exist. "*Maite zaitut*," she told me in Basque. "I love you." She pronounced the zee in the Spanish way.

"Did I say it right?"

I said yes.

"It's wonderful," she said. "How well you write, you've stunned me." After many similar remarks, she asked me if I knew where she was. Of course I told her I didn't. How was I to know?

"I'm lying on my bed, and my thighs are burning." I couldn't even swallow. I was astonished by her behavior, and proud of the effectiveness of my writing. The book I had been reading slipped from my hands.

"And what are you doing?" she asked.

"Reading *Neurosis and Genius*," I answered, thinking it was the book that suited my nature best. But she didn't seem to be in the mood for such details. "When can you come?" she whispered. I said I didn't know, that I would come whenever she liked. I couldn't think. Without giving me time to react, she said, "Take the train at noon and call me from the hotel as soon as you arrive," and hung up.

Of course I couldn't do anything else that morning. At the time I was trying to write something about literature and neurosis, encouraged by Sedano. The idea was to demonstrate the extent to which literature can be said to be a neurotic game. I was to work on the lives and works of great neurotic writers, and Sedano was to analyze the effect of their neurotic traits on their writing. Like most of Sedano's projects, however, this one served as an excuse for several dinners and many more drinks, and neither of us got much actual writing done. To tell the truth, we didn't even arrive at a final selection of writers, among other things because Sedano sees a neurotic in every writer. We did read a lot about the subject, though. What comes first, neurosis or literature? Does the neurotic write because he's a neurotic or does he become a neurotic because he writes? That's what the book I mentioned to Eugenia, *Neurosis and Genius,* is all about.

I tried to force myself to work, but it was impossible. I read the previous day's papers and smoked one cigarette after the other, as I usually do at difficult moments, and at noon ate a sandwich. Then I put my toothbrush, a shirt, two pairs of underwear and my notes on *Creative Madness* in a bag and set out for Norte train station.

The Talgo, the fast train from Irun to Madrid, makes me claustrophobic, especially in the last hour of the journey. I was exhausted when I arrived in Madrid, and my unease had increased considerably. For that reason, I took a room in the Chamartín hotel, close to the station. I was in the habit of staying there, since it allowed me to get rid of my suitcases as soon as possible, and because its close proximity to the station gave me the feeling that I was already on my journey back. So I called her from the Chamartín and she told me she would come in half an hour. That only gave me time to brush my teeth, which was fortunate, since having to wait longer would have intensified my anxiety. As she hadn't specified where to meet, I decided to wait for her outside. She turned up ahead of time, smartly dressed and with her face neatly made up. She was wearing a very tight, green, velvety dress, and white tights with silver stripes, which were in fashion at the time, if I'm not mistaken. I think her lipstick was white, too—a glossy white, for that was also fashionable at one point—but they were still very sensual. Eugenia was in the splendor of maturity.

Smiling, she only said, "*Hola*" and kissed me on the lips for the first time. Then she took my hand and pulled me into the hotel. "Shall we go up?"

The idea that I was about to do something I'd soon regret flashed across my mind, and I was suddenly overcome by a sense of guilt that's probably the result of our generation's repressive education, which taught us that the price of a moment's happiness is eternal damnation. We were brought up to believe this and haven't been able to forget it, though in general the clergymen who educated us have. And apparently our saintly mothers don't remember the old sermons very well either, if even half of what people say about widows' clubs is true.

I've never asked Sedano to explain this guilt complex, but I'm sure he'd link it to my neurosis. The point is that I had all this in mind as we walked to the escalator holding hands, and that obviously these weren't the most appropriate thoughts for the occasion. She started to kiss me on the escalator, fervently, nearly out of breath, and continued in the same way when we got to the corridor, though it's very open and illuminated. But she didn't seem to care, and that surprised me. I had thought we'd have dinner first, and a drink or two in a quiet place, but apparently she had no time for preambles.

I won't speak at length about this. I thought by this point that she wouldn't take time for even a quick look around the room, but it seems I know very little about women, because she said something I can't remember about my lack of attention to detail; something about there being pleasanter places in Madrid than a station hotel.

The room was modern-looking, with white Formica furniture and spherical lamps. Everything was impersonal and aseptic. I was about to tell her that, after all, it was a four-star hotel, but in the end I excused myself by telling her it was just a habit, that I stayed there only because when I traveled on the night train I could leave my bags there and take a shower right away. And as I was saying this I realized I should have done so on this occasion too: the journey had been very hot. I told her that. But she didn't let go of me.

"It doesn't matter," she said.

Nevertheless, I had to admit to myself that the gap between reality and the scene I had described in my note was too wide, and that made me feel guilty again. I should at least have had a bottle of champagne ready. With all this preying on my mind, I even feared the worst would happen. But it didn't go all that badly, considering it was our first time together.

She said it had been wonderful, but I guess what she really felt was that for the first time it hadn't gone too badly. She also told me the lines I had written her were wonderful. She got out of bed and reached for her hand-bag. It never ceases to surprise me how quickly women lose their inhibitions about showing their bodies once they have undressed in front of a man. Eugenia is one of those women who look thinner when they are naked. I told her so, that she looked younger without her clothes on. She didn't seem embarrassed; she came back to bed and started reading my note. There I was, holding a bottle of champagne bedecked with pearls of water, two glasses in my pockets; and there she was, her thighs afire amid silk sheets. At that moment, when Eugenia read it aloud, I felt it was well written. Above all, it gave one the feeling of having been written with ease, happily so to speak. It sounded quite natural. She repeated how wonderful it was, that it was the most beautiful present she had ever been given, and that she was proud to have inspired such words.

I ended up believing my text was good, and again regretted not having been more attentive, at least when choosing the hotel, for I hadn't been able to match reality with fiction.

"It's you," I told her. "You inspire the best kind of writing."

To some extent I did believe what I was saying, and I think she did too. Anyway, she pounced on me again with renewed force, moving her body with the lithe vivacity of small women. I did what I could, and she told me again that it had been wonderful. I don't know why, but she sounded more truthful when she said it about my writing. I didn't reply. She seemed at a loss for something to say. In the end, she volunteered to find a room in a cozy hotel next time. "I know a very nice one."

"I like the Chamartín," I told her maliciously, "because its name derives from *etxe-Martin*, or 'Martin's house' in Basque."

"Really?"

"Really." With the help of etymology, half the world could be Basque.

We both fell silent for a moment, wrapped in the night, gazing at the reflections of the streetlights on the ceiling. I was asking myself when the right moment would be to suggest going out for dinner, when she said, "What's wrong with you Basques?" as she had many times before. Only this time she lovingly put her hand on my forehead, as one does to a sick child. I told her nothing was wrong, at least not with me, and brushed her hand away, too brusquely perhaps. The only thing that was wrong was that I was eager to get to any of the bars around the station and have a plate of Jabugo ham while reading a book.

She seemed to read my thoughts. She told me it was getting late, and got up and went to the bathroom. Once in there, she asked me if I had a comb. I told her to have a look in my toilet bag, and lay back waiting for her to come out. She wasn't long. I sat up to tell her I'd see her to her car, but she said there was no need. I remember well how, before leaving, she kissed my forehead.

"*Maite zaitut*," she said. "Am I saying it right?" I told her yes, she said it very well. When she left she said, "*Hasta mañana*," probably because that was what she normally said.

In any case, I took the train back to San Sebastián the following morning.

She kept calling me every day for a long time. The first time, she told me she was very upset that I had left Madrid so soon, and more so because I had left without saying goodbye. I didn't try very hard to come up with an excuse. I simply told her I had run into an unexpected problem. Another time she wanted to make it clear that she wasn't the kind of woman who went to bed with just anyone; that she felt something special for me, and that it was because of my note. From what she said, I gathered she often reread it. "I've got it right here," she would say, "I keep it with me all the time." And she would describe how I would come in with a bottle of champagne in my hand and two glasses in my pockets, and how she would be waiting for me, naked, lying on the silk sheets with her thighs on fire, and all the rest of it. I ended up switching on the answering machine so she wouldn't catch me unawares, but nevertheless she kept calling for a long time, leaving pathetic messages telling me to at least write her a line, until one day she stopped phoning.

I met Victoria in London about a year or two later. I was in London because, having been appointed its Spanish delegate by the psychoanalytic association to which he belonged, Sedano had managed to get me invited to a seminar on Literature and Neurosis at their first European Congress. However, I knew very little about the subject apart from what I had gathered from our discussions about our book on "creative madness," which we hadn't begun to write yet, and to be honest, I hadn't taken the time to read anything else. Nevertheless, staying silent wasn't a big problem when one was with Sedano's friends; the real difficulty was getting a single word in edgeways into their cryptic discourse.

Sedano and I were sitting in the restaurant on the second or third floor of the National Theatre, along with a French psychoanalyst who said he had been analyzed by Lacan, and an Argentinean who introduced himself as the author of *Metonymy and Pleasure*. We were at the theater to see a performance of *Waiting for Godot*. They had initially wanted to stage *Hamlet*, but that had turned out to be impossible due to scheduling problems, so they were putting on *Godot* instead.

I didn't agree with their choice, since in my opinion *Godot* has more to do with reason than with unreason. So I told them that Beckett was an example to be followed, if not for analysts then at least for writers, and that I thought it an offence to include him in a program about neurosis. After all, Beckett didn't send his psychoanalyst to hell for nothing.

Of course, I didn't expect my objections to be taken into account. But I stood my ground firmly, saying that I definitely wouldn't stay for the performance—which would allow me to take the afternoon off to walk around London and preserve my dignity at the same time.

We were having our dessert when Victoria entered the restaurant. Her tall, slender figure didn't go unnoticed. She was the type of woman who seems to be made for wearing a wide straw hat. Her clothing was discreet but very elegant, the kind even the most untrained eye would recognize as refined and expensive. She was wearing a black trouser suit mottled with pale blue, and flat black shoes.

She gave our conversation a new turn, or rather, she silenced the Argentinean who was rattling on about Gide's oral fixation. According to Sedano, she was one of those English beauties who are very rare, and whose beauty approaches perfection. The French psychiatrist for his part pointed out that she didn't look English, at least her clothes didn't. What matters, however, is that they both had to turn around to look at her, whereas, happily, the Argentinean and I could watch her at our leisure.

She sat straight, gracefully holding her svelte body erect, separating her Dover sole from the bone with great ease and naturalness, even though she must have been aware that everyone was staring at her; at our table, at least, nobody took their eyes off her. I had ordered the sole as well and, taking the coincidence to be a good sign, told myself that if we also chose the same dessert, it would mean that we were soon to meet. I knew, however, that the only purpose of such a thought was to delude myself, precisely to avoid taking any steps that might actually lead to meeting her. After all, though the dessert menu wasn't long, the odds were against her also ordering champagne sorbet with fruits of the forest. This is something I often do to avoid making decisions: if she ordered the crêpes with Armagnac I had been about to choose, or a tasty-looking apple pie, or a tempting pudding, in short, anything but the sorbet I eventually opted for, I would already have an excuse to avoid the risk of failure. And even if she did choose the champagne sorbet with fruits of the forest, I would have time to make up another excuse.

By doing mental arithmetic, for instance. I have this tendency they call arithmomania, which in my case consists in counting two by two, especially when I'm faced with an unpleasant task, or seven by seven, until I get to a certain limit which I can then extend as much as I want. Sedano says this kind of thing is an obsessive-compulsive symptom that shelters the neurotic from his inner conflicts. Its purpose is to free him of the burden of having to decide, or to postpone the moment of decision for as long as possible.

Though Sedano's theories often seem like baseless speculations to me—for example when he talks about wanting to preserve the mother's phallus—I have to confess that he sometimes says very sensible things. In any case, I was quite pleased when the conference secretary appeared to tell us the play was about to begin. The Frenchman and the Argentinean were to introduce the play, and as Sedano was on the organizing committee, he had to take his place in the front row in good time. So the three of them got ready to leave. I told them again that I wouldn't help them coax Beckett onto Lacan's couch, and with great dignity declared that I had decided to boycott the play.

When they left I began to look for the most suitable phrase to introduce myself to Victoria, though I knew perfectly well that there was no real point, since I would never have the nerve to approach her. I was finding it hard to choose a single phrase, for I knew that on such occasions the first words are usually crucial. In the end, I decided that either, "May I join you?" or perhaps, "Would you mind if I join you?" would be best.

It takes some know-how, though, to approach a woman, glass in hand, and ask her, in English: "Do you mind if I join you?" And I don't have it. Only once was I able to approach a girl like that, out of the blue. It was in Oxford, where I was doing a postgraduate course in literature. Though I had never talked to her, I had seen her around the college, and she must have seen me too. The circumstances were therefore as favorable as could be expected. I approached her after class and asked her if I could walk her home. "Who cares what I say," she answered, "you'll do as you wish anyway." So I decided to accompany her, but we didn't speak to each other the whole way, and when we got to her door I simply didn't stop. I kept walking for a long time, until I got to a neighborhood full of terraced houses, where dogs barked viciously at me from behind fences.

I didn't hear Victoria's dessert order well, but I did catch her say something about fruits. Though she might simply have ordered the seasonal fruit, which was also on the menu, I took it for granted that our choices were about to coincide again, and my heart started beating wildly.

I didn't have to wait long for my doubts to be cleared up: the waitress appeared a few moments later carrying a sorbet with forest fruits. "Here you are, madam."

"Thank you," Victoria said. She looked at me and smiled, aware that I was staring at her. I was unable to meet her gaze and quickly pretended to be reading something.

I had to admit that this coincidence—the fact that we had both chosen the same two courses—must mean something, though I didn't want to think about what it obliged me to do. It could be of great help in breaking the ice, because it gave me the opportunity to walk over and tell her, "I've realized that we agree, at least about food," and that I'd like to know if we also agreed on other things. I was very tempted by this impulse, but hamstrung by my lack of courage, and this conflict of feelings made me break out in a heavy sweat.

In this kind of situation our brain is usually unable to think. We're animals, physically and biochemically prepared to escape from frightening situations: our blood pressure lowers so we won't lose much blood if we're wounded; we sweat so our skin is slick in case our adversary grabs us. I grabbed the table with both hands to prevent myself from running away. In the end, to calm myself down, I decided to enjoy the presence of this woman I still didn't know, at least for the moment, while she finished her dessert and had her coffee—if she had a coffee—though, of course, that would mean breaking the promise I had made to myself.

It wasn't a difficult decision to make, and even though it meant missing the opportunity to meet her, I eventually calmed down. That's the good thing about disillusionment: it brings peace, calm. Besides, experience teaches us to handle frustration; I only had to imagine what it would have been like if, after walking up to her with my glass in my hand and telling her, "I see we agree" and so on, she told me that was no miracle given the brevity of the dessert menu, or couldn't understand my English ("Sorry?"), or simply politely asked me to leave her alone.

Thus encouraged by having freed myself from all my burdensome resolutions, I decided to raise my head. I was curious about whether she would order a coffee. I told myself she wouldn't. I reckoned she wouldn't have tea either; she would finish her dessert, pay her bill and leave, after drinking a glass of water at most. But this time I didn't promise myself to do anything if I guessed right.

She was finishing her dessert. The most incredible thing was that, though her body, her movements, her good manners and her beauty (for beauty always seems distant to us, in the same way that blue eyes seem cold) might have given her a proud air, there was something about her that suggested she was nice, humble and friendly. At one point she looked at me over the glass of water she was about to sip from, and her emerald eyes brightened with a faint smile. They were so vivid that the color of her irises seemed to occupy her entire eyes. They were the kind of eyes that usually can't smile—but Victoria's could.

I smiled back, or at least that was what my brain ordered my face to do. I'm not sure I would have been able to remain that way for much longer, with my lips stretched, gazing into her eyes... Luckily the waiter got in our way. He picked up a napkin from the floor, turned to Victoria and asked her if she would like a cup of coffee. "Some coffee, Madam?"

I didn't have time to indicate the reply I would have liked her to make, since she answered in the negative right away. "Just the bill, please." Although I was happy that my intuition was right again, I felt nervous, because I knew I had little time to make her acquaintance—the time it would take for the waiter to bring the bill and for her to pay. I was so deep in these thoughts that I didn't realize the waiter was talking to me, let alone understand what he was telling me. I eventually noticed him: he was emphasizing his pronunciation slowly and exaggeratedly: "Excuse me sir."

"He's asking if you'd like something else," she said in Spanish. "I guess it's the end of his shift."

They probably both took me for a fool. I told the waiter I was all right, that I didn't want anything, and turned to Victoria: "Thanks, I was miles away."

But realizing that this was a perfect opportunity to make her acquaintance made me very anxious, and though there were many things I might have said, such as asking her where she came from, since she spoke such good Spanish, there I was, unable to decide where to begin, like a starving person suddenly given free choice from a table full of delicious dishes. I was also worried about what we had been saying about her, thinking she wouldn't understand us; I had in mind at least one obscene remark by Sedano, who, though he might not be an obsessive neurotic, can certainly be vulgar and indecent. And even though all our remarks, however inappropriate, had been intended to praise her beauty, I nevertheless began to gather up all my papers and put them in my Creative Madness folder, resolved to leave the place as quickly as possible.

But of course, while I was doing this, I dropped half the sheets. I was kneeling on the floor when I heard Victoria's voice again: "You did the right thing defending Beckett against those people."

Her Spanish was fluent, and she modulated her voice like an actress. Her voice was soft and clear, as if she were right beside me. I raised my head from under the table, but all I could offer by way of reply was a faint smile. I stayed where I was, kneeling on the floor, and saw her take her change, slip her purse into her bag, and put her jacket on.

"*Bueno, hasta otra,*" she said, and I echoed, "*Sí, hasta otra,*" looking at her as she walked toward the stairs and disappeared. I picked up my things and began to count to thirty, the time I thought it would take her to get to the exit. I'd made up my mind to catch her unawares on the street. I'd follow her for a few feet, come up beside her and say, "*Hola.*" Just like that. Or perhaps I would say, "*Hola,*" and then, "we met at the restaurant."

I was out of breath when I got to the first floor; in the end I had feared I would lose sight of her if I counted to thirty. Suddenly I saw her standing in the queue in the café. I took a tray and cup and lined up behind her. She turned and said, "*Hola,*" as if she had known me all her life, and that was when I realized for the first time that Victoria had the gift of making difficult things easy. She told me she liked the atmosphere on the ground floor, but that the food was better in the upstairs restaurant. When the cashier asked if we were together, I told her we were. I think my voice broke. She let me pay, but I couldn't do it without dropping my change on the floor. I was therefore on my knees again, picking up the coins, when she suggested that we take a seat by the window.

I agreed, of course. Outside, there was a secondhand book fair and a group of boys were doing tricks with their bikes. I could see the Courtauld Institute on the other side of the Thames. Around us, middle-aged men and women carefully read their theater programs and filled in their membership forms while sipping cups of coffee or tea. It was easy to imagine the riverside crowded with people carrying briefcases, and that made the theater seem even quieter. She told me that if I was keen on drama there was a very good specialist library in the theater. I told her I wasn't. She said that, to be honest, she wasn't either.

We asked each other the same question at the same time ("Where are you from?") and gave the same answer ("From San Sebastián") with a laugh. She was from San Sebastián but had studied in Bayonne as a child and spent most of her life away from the Basque Country, except for the two years she had wasted at law school in San Sebastián. She didn't tell me her name at first. She told me she worked for a couple of art galleries in Paris, where she spent most of the year, and that her job was to import artworks from London, mainly to Madrid. I later found out that she quite easily sold the objects she had bought for twice the price, just because they had been bought at Christie's in London.

"So you're a psychoanalyst," she said.

And without giving me time to answer, she jokily admitted that she had been listening to us carefully; not that she had needed to, given the volume of our conversation. I told her she was wrong. The other three were psychoanalysts, but I wasn't. I decided to introduce myself as a writer. "I write." I told her. I was in doubt whether to tell her I was a writer, but in the end I just told her, "I write."

"I'm not sure what's worse."

"Worse?"

"Being a writer or a psychoanalyst," she had to clarify, and I was afraid she'd think I was dimwitted. For her,

writers and psychoanalysts were of the same ilk, but analysts had sadistic tendencies, whereas we leaned more
toward masochism. Without giving it much thought, I
resolved to agree with her.

"And what do you write about?"

I told her the truth: that I mostly wrote commissioned works, among which *The Basque Country: Landscape and Gastronomy* was the best known, but that I also
wrote novels. I specified that I wrote in Basque.

"How interesting!" she said in Basque. She said was
sorry she hadn't read any of my writing. In fact, she hardly ever read anything in Basque. Her Basque (she had
learned it at law school in San Sebastián and later
improved it at the Basque Center in Paris) was limited but
correct. When I congratulated her on it, she told me it
was mere illusion: a multilingual person's ability to con-
struct decent sentences with very few means.

I pointed out that she hadn't told me her name yet,
and we exchanged names. "Victoria." I told her that it
reminded me of San Sebastián: the romantic area, the yellowish color of the sandstone houses in the twilight, the
Victoria Eugenia Theater, and the golden reflections of
the lights on the Kursaal bridge trembling on the surface
of the river.

"Look at you," she answered, "three days away from
home and you're already eaten up by nostalgia."

I told her it wasn't true, that they were simply images
her name evoked.

"Well, I'd say I'm more of a Victoria Station type.
Anyway, San Sebastián isn't what it used to be, though
you people don't want to see it..." She opened her pack of
sugar and poured half of it in her coffee. "Besides, they

haven't presented any shows at the Victoria Eugenia Theater since they built the Kursaal auditorium."

"The Kursaal, of course…" I wanted to say something, but I didn't know exactly what.

"Do you like it?" She seemed very interested in my opinion.

I didn't dare say either that I did or didn't; I simply shrugged my shoulders.

"I feel sorry for the lampposts on the bridge," she said. "They were so big, almost like lighthouses, and now they seem small with that huge building in the background." She stirred her coffee, deep in thought. "Some of my friends can't understand how I can be so upset by such a trifle, and I don't understand it myself sometimes, but it's the same with my crow's feet: they're a trifle to others, but they worry me when I look at myself in the mirror."

"It's true that you shouldn't worry."

I don't know if she understood my reply. She put an elbow on the table and rested her chin on her cupped hand.

"Perhaps we have an oedipal relationship with that beautiful city of ours. Don't you think so?

"Maybe."

"After all, at one time San Sebastián was all detail, balance, perfection." She smiled, sipped her coffee, put the cup on its saucer and smiled again. "Nevertheless, our San Sebastián is still a very beautiful city. Anyway…"

She said "anyway" twice in an attempt to revive the conversation, looking at me expectantly. I couldn't find a way to start an interesting exchange, because I couldn't get Sedano's words out of my mind: "In his encounter with the Other, the obsessive neurotic fails."

When he's with me, Sedano acts as if all the world's neurotics were before him, and to tell you the truth I think I had fewer problems when I didn't know anything about my neurosis. I was more natural. I mean that I used to handle my obsessive neurosis with more spontaneity when I wasn't so aware of it. In any case, the real problem is time: you feel time fly away and you want to say something witty, interesting or genuine without giving the other person time to think you're dull. Haste is what ruins it all. If you know you have time you can say everything— about time itself, about the trees, whatever—as long as you can find the right words.

I dried my palms on my knees and, when I dared to look at her, I got the notion that she wanted to leave, thinking I was a bore. "Don't leave," I said to myself. I suppose I must have been thinking about Eugenia, because I had also been very embarrassed when I met her. I don't know. In any case, just for the sake of saying something, I suddenly asked her if she had ever been to Aranjuez. She simply answered that she had. I mean it didn't strike her as odd that I had asked her precisely about Aranjuez, of all the places in the world.

"Aranjuez is beautiful, too."

"Yes. *Aranjuez mon amour.*"

Her voice indicated boredom. I was sure of it. But I couldn't help asking her about Eugénie. There was something about my affair with Eugenia that was driving me to repeat, word for word, the conversation we had had on the day I met her. On that occasion Eugenia hadn't believed what I had said about the armpits of the waitresses at Eugénie.

"Eugenié Les Bains?" She was probably quite surprised by my line of enquiry. "It's a health spa where they serve dietetic meals... I haven't been there for a long time."

It was obvious that telling her about the waitresses made no sense at all, but I felt compelled to tell her the anecdote, even though I knew it was completely foolish, and worse still, in very bad taste. And of course, no good story can come from that kind of motivation. So I told her the story, the one I have told so many times with such little success (deservedly so), but when I raised both my hands as if to uncover the imaginary dishes, it was she who said: "And a stench of onion spreads all over the restaurant."

Astonished, I asked her whether it had happened to her.

"Well it wasn't difficult to guess the ending, but I've seen it happen, yes."

The fact that she had spoiled my anecdote didn't frustrate me a bit. On the contrary, I realized that something that Eugenia had found implausible was a matter of personal experience with Victoria; an experience which, moreover, she shared with me. I took it for a good sign, cheered up, and ventured to ask her if she was doing anything that afternoon. She told me she wasn't. "Just losing myself in the streets," she said.

She seemed to be fond of walking the streets of London with nothing to do, alternating between the bustle of people and traffic and the quiet of squares and alleys. We went outside and walked along the riverside, going nowhere in particular. We crossed the footbridge and walked up to Trafalgar Square. It was crowded with people and gray pigeons and surrounded by red buses. "You can still feel like you're at the center of the world here," she said. The monument to the victorious Lord Nelson reminded me of Trafalgar in Cadiz: a long beach swept by the wind and the green sea, that still seems to hold the memory of defeat. Though that's where Nelson died, he's not there; he's at the top of the tall column in Trafalgar square. After all, it's impossible to be in two different places at the same time. This is what I tried to explain to Victoria, that I'm not a good traveler: I can't really enjoy being anywhere, since I'm always missing some other place. She told me an aunt of hers had the same problem. Her children were in Venezuela, and her sisters and brothers were in San Sebastián. The husband was also in Venezuela, but apparently that didn't bother her much, she said laughing. The funny thing is that when she was in Venezuela, the woman would spend the day crying because she missed her brothers and sisters, and did just the same in San Sebastián because she missed her children.

I told her I didn't know whether I was quite that bad, but added that, in any event, standing in front of such monuments to imperial victory made me feel like creating my own memorial to defeat.

"Come on," she said suddenly, and took me by the hand.

She did it spontaneously. She pulled me down Pall Mall to St James's Square. Along the way, I tried to interpret what that gesture of taking my hand might mean. I didn't know what to make of it, and decided not to hold out much hope. That bodily contact could simply be a way of opening the door to friendship, and indeed of closing it to other kinds of relationships. Experience had shown me that the women who are most extroverted when you first meet them are usually the most inhibited when it comes to entering into intimate relationships, and that they feel frustrated and offended when men interpret their friendly gestures as seduction strategies.

Once at St James's we stopped at the second building on the side of the square leading to Duke of York Street. She climbed the steps to the front door and rang the bell. I stayed on the sidewalk. "This is Victoria," she said in English, "I'm bringing a visitor; it'll only take a minute." Then she pushed open the door and motioned at me to come up.

We crossed a gallery, past a staircase that smelled of wax, and went through a small glass doorway into an enclosed courtyard paved with stone. In the middle of the courtyard stood a bronze sculpture. It was composed of two life-sized figures, both nude and both very graceful: an angel with fallen wings, standing on one foot, holding the body of a soldier in its arms. The soldier held out the broken sword of defeat.

"Do you like it?" she asked.

I thought it was beautiful, truly moving, and told her so.

"In the nineteenth century, bronze was often used to make real rubbish, but I really like this composition."

We were alone at the foot of the statue, and only the flight of pigeons could be heard from time to time as they flew from one window to another. To her knowledge there were at least three reproductions of the same statue. One in Paris, in Montholon square, and another in Bordeaux, by the cathedral. Its name was *Gloria Victis*: Glory to the Defeated.

"There it is, the monument to defeat you were longing for." She moved back slowly until she touched the wall, to gain a better perspective. I did the same, searching for something to say. "It's certainly beautiful," was all I could come up with.

"Nelson is quite pitiful up there at the zenith of victory, all alone. This beautiful soldier's defeat, how sweet it is!" She turned to face me, smiling. "You agree, don't you?"

"Maybe," I answered.

"Sure you do; you love the aesthetics of defeat."

I was tempted to ask her who she was talking about when she spoke again: "It was a lord who had this put here," she said, gesturing at the bronze couple, "but there's no agreement on his reasons for doing so. Some say he did it because his cricket team had lost a tournament, but there are also those who say, in better faith, that he erected it because a friend of his had stolen his wife."

I had no way of telling whether she was joking, for she turned and headed toward the street. "*La douce défaite*," she told me, "Sweet defeat. Surely, you must know something about it?"

I asked her why she said that.

"You'll get angry if I tell you."

I promised her I wouldn't get angry. "I won't. I promise."

"When one gets drawn into the aesthetics of defeat, any interest in victory vanishes."

She said it in Spanish, probably because she found it difficult to convey the idea in Basque. "You're a melancholic," she went on. "Most of you Basques are, and if you're at war it's only because you pine for defeat. You love its aesthetics and you wouldn't know how to adapt to the winner's role." She laughed to show me she was joking. "It's very hard to stand up there, on the pinnacle of victory, like Nelson. How sweet, instead, to lie in the arms of the beauteous angel of defeat!" She waved her arms in the air as though mimicking the flight of an angel, then, when she noticed I was deep in thought, let them fall. "Come on, cheer up; I'll be your London guide," she said, speaking Basque again, and set out with a quick step. We were back in Pall Mall, in view of Nelson once again.

"The column is 52 meters high and was designed by William Railton," she said hurriedly, more like a schoolgirl than a guide. "See how professional I am?"

She suggested going to the National Gallery for a walk and another cup of coffee. I replied that it would be a good idea to get away from the crowds. "Wait," she said, putting a hand on my chest to stop me, though I hadn't moved.

"I've just remembered I ordered some books at the Tate Gallery for a client in Madrid. I ought to pick them up. Do you mind?"

I told her I didn't, of course; that I didn't give a damn where I went, as long as it was with her. I pretended to be joking, but it was perfectly true. I don't know if she suspected it.

We went down Whitehall. At the junction with Downing Street, there was a demonstration against the family benefit reform. We crossed Parliament Square and walked down Millbank to the Tate Britain Gallery. I don't know how long it took us; an hour or so, perhaps. It was a very pleasant walk. She told me she had wanted to be a painter, but that at eighteen she had suddenly realized she was unable to invent anything new and had given it up. She said she remembered that day perfectly. She hadn't picked up a brush since then.

"Only those who've given up painting understand its importance," she said.

"Possibly. They often say that about writing too."

"You haven't stopped writing, though."

"I haven't."

I said it without much conviction, for I remembered that I still had to finish the second half of *Landscape and Gastronomy*. "No, I haven't," I repeated, trying to convince myself.

She added, "Fortunately."

"Yes, fortunately."

She was two steps above me by the entrance to the Tate. "Lucky you," she said, beckoning me to follow her.

Once inside, she asked me what I'd like to see, and I desperately searched for an appropriate answer. "We'll have to go for Turner," I told her, "though I like Constable better." I didn't waste the opportunity to show that I knew Constable had spent all his life painting the same tree. She in turn told me that most artists are always painting the same tree.

We crossed the foyer, and I caught a glimpse of one of Chillida's iron pieces in the adjoining room. There it was: so solid, so peculiar. Unmistakable, and above all familiar. I told her I felt at home whenever I was near one of Chillida's sculptures. "Yes, we've come to identify ourselves with his work. Or perhaps," shrugging her shoulders, "he's the one who's come to identify with us; he's taken root in something that's common to all of us..." Without finishing the sentence, she turned back and pointed at a stone sculpture by Moore. "Nevertheless, Moore is also my home."

She was walking a couple of steps ahead of me, without paying much attention to me. She didn't look at most of the paintings either. Only now and then would she stop in front of one to admire it more closely. She got very near them, with her eyes half closed, apparently to examine the details better. It was as though she were walking up and down a market, as when I go around the vegetable and fish stalls, trying to tell the Tudela and Murcia artichokes apart, or trying to guess which hakes are from Hondarribia Bay and which are Namibian.

I can't recall exactly which paintings she stopped to scrutinize, but I remember her standing before a Cézanne and saying, "Everything is in Cézanne," as, apparently, Picasso had said before her. She also repeated that other quote: when a painting captures order and luminosity, it means that the same order and clarity exist in the artist's mind, and that he or she is aware of their importance. It was Matisse who said it. So she told me. She sometimes spoke in French, searching for a more precise formulation, but she said this in English. When I asked her why, she replied that as a child she was given several books in *The Artist Speaks* series as a present and had liked them so much that she had learned whole sentences by heart: quotes by Monet, Picasso, Renoir, Matisse, but only in their English versions. Since then she preferred to read writings by the artists themselves, rather than critics. As she saw it, critics were obscure and cryptic, whereas great artists were transparent and lucid. "All that is not useful in the picture is detrimental." Matisse's color rectangles on a canvas. Green, blue, fuchsia, black.

I didn't dare ask why she got so close to the paintings, fearing it might be common knowledge, but I felt the need to say something, to avoid staying silent all the time, so I told her I disagreed. As I saw it, painters painted precisely because that was their mode of expression; if they were able to express the same thing in words they would surely do so. Instead of painting, they would just say what they had to say. She turned to me and smiled. "Painters, and I in particular, aren't clever at translating their feelings into words." She sounded like a child reciting a lesson. "They paint because they like it, but that doesn't make them incapable of putting their reflections on their work into words." She spoke with a solemnity she hadn't shown until then, and it seemed to me by the way she frowned when she looked at me that she wondered whether I was able to understand what she was saying. "Anyway, I'd rather listen to an artist, however fumbling he or she may be, than to some prattling critic who hasn't gone through the experience."

I didn't reply, since the topic didn't really interest me. As I see it, artists also talk a lot of nonsense. Besides, she had started walking again, and I hurried after her. We passed through several rooms without even stopping to have a look around, until we got to the Turner wing. "Here are your Turners," she told me.

There they were: the Venetian landscapes of the old
and near-blind Turner, covered by a white and yellow veil
that made them look wholly abstract. I tried hard to think
of something original to say, something that would show
her I wasn't completely ignorant of art. I stopped before
the painting that seemed the most veiled to me, and
asked: "Is this an intellectual development, the culmination of a move from realism to abstraction, or is it simply
a sign of Turner's physical decay?"

"Well, I don't know, and I must admit I don't care. I
don't understand all the morbid speculation that seems to
surround it. Was Michelangelo aware that his going
beyond the figurative in his slaves series was leading him
toward abstraction, or did he leave them as they are simply because he was fed up and didn't feel like finishing
them? Does it really matter?"

We were alone in the exhibition room. I could make
out a gloomy Venice before me, through white and yellow
patches. I could also tell, by her voice, that she didn't like
the English artist, and I regretted having told her I wanted to see his paintings. Moreover, I realized I had nothing
to say about them. Had we gone to the National Gallery
instead, where we would surely have seen Leonardo's car-
toon, I would have had the opportunity to mention all the
curious things I knew about it, and there were quite a few,
because I had read Freud's essay, "Leonardo da Vinci and
a Memory of His Childhood" when I was researching *Creative Madness.*

I was getting weary of the museum, and remembered
that we had decided to go to the Tate because she had to
pick up some books at the store. So I asked her if she had
forgotten. She had, and thanked me for reminding her.

Perhaps if I hadn't reminded her I wouldn't even have discovered who Rossetti was, and things would have turned out differently. Perhaps our relationship wouldn't have ended the way it did. But I did it, I reminded her.

"Don't forget you had to pick some books."

"Do you mind if we pick them up right away, so I don't forget again?" she asked.

We walked back to the shop. I had a look at the post-cards while she was at the counter. Her order had already come in, and she got the books. "See what kinds of errands I get sent on?" she said when she approached me. She had been asked to buy the books by an old man in Madrid, who had previously asked her to find a painter who could copy all of Rossetti's works. It was obvious that Victoria didn't like the Pre-Raphaelites. She took one of the books out of the bag. The cover illustration was a reproduction of a very famous painting: the model Rossetti used most, in profile, with a pomegranate in her hand. The outstanding detail, apart from the woman's melancholic beauty, was that the pomegranate was partly peeled, exposing its red seeds and giving it the appearance of entrails. Its title was *The Pre-Raphaelite Vision*.

Regrettably, I told her, "They were on to something, those Pre-Raphaelites." I guess I didn't want to seem too meek or conciliatory. I wanted to show her that I had my own criteria. Though I didn't know much about these painters, I was quite interested. I liked the atmosphere they created in their paintings, but I should confess that what really attracted me may have been their models. Women with the beauty of Greek statues: limpid features, long strong necks, fleshy well-shaped lips. Their gaze also resembles that of statues: disheartened, lost in the dream-like landscapes that surround them. I wasn't overly enthusiastic by the reproductions, but there was something attractive and revealing about them. She put the book back in the bag.

"Tell me what you like about them."

"They're not the worst painters of the nineteenth century," I said to defend myself.

I didn't want to annoy her either. Moreover, I realized their works hadn't aged well. They were too stiff, like *papier mâché*. But I didn't want to give in. "They're very literary," I told her, just to say something.

"Literary," she said heatedly. "Illustrative, you mean."

I know it sounds macho, but it's true: seeing her like that, on the verge of anger, made her even more beautiful to me. If I liked them, she said, it was precisely because they restricted art's role to illustrating literature. They painted Dante and Shakespeare, but they had nothing of their own to say. "And if they do, they're impenetrable."

We were at the other entrance, outside the shop. I thought we were leaving at last, but she said, "Come on, follow me," and quickly walked inside again. We went up one floor, through several rooms, until she finally stopped in front of John Everet Millais' *Ophelia*, that stunning woman floating in a pond, dead, wearing a dress which seems made of heliotropes and which merges with the flowers on the surface of the water. I later discovered that the woman was Elizabeth Siddal, Rossetti's wife, and that at the time of the painting she was twenty-two. The painting is beautiful, whatever Victoria may say, and it's obvious that it was a source of inspiration for Klimt. Standing in front of it I had the revelatory sensation that we get when we see the originals of works we are familiar with through reproductions, as when we see celluloid film stars in the flesh.

"It isn't *ugly*," I told her.

"*Douce est la mort qui vient en bien aimant.* They're so priggish, so morbid and macabre. *Des vrais salauds.* They probably kept the poor thing mercilessly soaked in water for more than a week, not caring whether she'd get tuberculosis."

Elizabeth Siddal, Rossetti's wife and the loveliest of the Pre-Raphaelite models, looks healthy. She has very fair skin, translucent but with a slight ruddiness, like many British women. Her mouth is open, revealing her front teeth, but her lips aren't purple: not the lips of someone who has drowned. The absent gaze of her blue eyes, however, is the exact image of death, without exaggeration.

"She looks too healthy," I answered maliciously. "She needs a bit of makeup to get the right waxy effect."

"Don't tease. You probably have a morbid mind, too. After all, most men do." Even though she tried to sound as if she were joking, she couldn't hide her true opinion. "Not to mention you psychoanalysts. Completely morbid, like priests in confessional boxes."

When I reminded her again that I wasn't a psychoanalyst but a writer, she repeated that she didn't know what was worse. I was about to ask her what she had against writers, but didn't, and now regret it, for I'm sure she does bear some grudge against us.

I acknowledged that the painting, or more precisely the literary work in question—for whatever she might say, there is literature in the Pre-Raphaelite paintings—touched some morbid strain within me. "Eros and Thanatos and all that," I told her. "But what's wrong with that?"

"Nothing at all. Only that you like sleeping beauties, sleeping or dead, it doesn't matter—lying among the flowers, waiting for you to rape them."

"Now that's going a bit too far."

"Only a bit," she said laughing.

She held the bag with the books up in front of me.

"Maybe my opinion is too much influenced by the fact that the lustful old man who asked me for these books likes the Pre-Raphaelites."

It was actually pleasant to argue with Victoria, because I didn't feel at risk of getting angry. In fact, to some extent I agreed with her way of seeing things. Whenever Sedano berated me for the intolerance and puritan fear that, according to him, anything pornographic produced in me, I used to take Victoria's stance. So on this occasion I was more or less playing the role Sedano would play with me. He used to boast about his taste for morbid and pornographic material, telling me that the ambiguous realm between life and death, or between pleasure and suffering—which I rejected because of my rigid morality—appealed to him. I told Victoria something along these lines.

"So I'm narrow-minded, then," she said.

A group of visitors had gotten between us, craning their necks to look at the painting more closely, and I didn't have the opportunity to tell her that I was the narrow-minded one. An idea reflected on by Doktor Glass, a character in a novel by the Swedish writer Hjalmar Söderberg, came back to me: "Why must we, in order to preserve our species and derive pleasure, use the same organs through which we evacuate foul matter every day? Wouldn't it be possible to do so through an act endowed with dignity and beauty, as well as the capability to provide intense pleasure?"

In a moment of weakness I once told Sedano that I agreed with this, something I've regretted many times since, for he often reminds me of it to make fun of my puritanism. He used to tell me that the need to separate love from desire was a neurotic trait, and that perhaps it was the Swedish novelist who had given Freud the idea for his essay, "The Most Prevalent Form of Degradation in Erotic Life." I didn't understand exactly what he meant, but I was sure that it's the emergence of sexuality that spells the end of childhood innocence, and that, like me, Victoria would have agreed with Doctor Glas' declaration after recounting how he felt as a child hearing a school-mate explain "what happens": "It seemed to me as if God himself had scribbled something filthy across the blue spring sky." I would have liked to recite these words to Victoria, for the sake of argument, to find out what she thought, or rather (though admitting it shames me), to follow the strategy of the filthy friars who educated me, if only to reject it, in order to be able to talk about sex.

In the end, I didn't share my thoughts with her. Not because I decided it would be wrong, but because an entire busload of Japanese tourists was now standing between us, and when we came together again, it was she who spoke. "Come," she told me, taking my hand again and pulling me to the back of the room.

The way she took my hand, so spontaneously, pleased me very much, since it showed that we could hold different views without getting angry at each other, and I enjoyed the intimacy that had arisen between us in the three hours we had been together.

We were standing in front of *Beata Beatrix*.

"Look at this poor girl," she said.

"I don't think you're narrow-minded," I wanted to clarify.

"I know, don't be such a fool," she said, looking at me with an affectionate smile. "Look at this other poor girl."

We were alone in front of the painting, and both fell silent looking at it: Elizabeth Siddal as Dante's Beatrice, at the moment of her death.

"I admit that these people broke with much of the conventional nineteenth-century junk, and that they cleared the way for symbolism and art nouveau, but to be honest they don't interest me one bit." She turned to face me, frowning again in that mischievous expression of hers. "And besides, Rossetti was a repulsive bastard. Look at that poor girl," she said again.

Beata Beatrix at death's door. A blaze of light emerging from the model's long hair spreads across the whole painting. Her face reflects at once ecstasy and calm. As in *Ophelia*, her mouth is open, showing her upper teeth, but here her ecstasy seems more sexual than religious, and her lips aren't fleshy as in Rossetti's other paintings: they are the thin lips of death. Though the painting is often said to

be Rossetti's best work, some think it macabre, a sign of
the author's necrophilia. According to Rossetti himself,
however, the painting represented the beloved at the
moment of her transition from earth to heaven.

Elizabeth Siddal died of a laudanum overdose. Laudanum is tincture of opium. According to the English
doctor Sydenham's formula, it was prepared by mixing
opium powder with alcohol. Saffron was then used to give
it color and Malaga wine essence to sweeten its scent.
Artists are said to have been particularly heavy users of it.

"The way she's biting her lower lip, she looks as if
she's about to start panting, like in erotic films."

Rossetti painted *Beata Beatrix* one or two years after
the death of his model and wife, in her memory. He did
it out of a feeling of remorse for leaving her alone in cold,
damp Chatham Place during her illness while he was out
visiting his mistresses. But then, we might also ask ourselves (and once we do, the painting becomes quite disturbing) whether her countenance, which Rossetti must
have known better than anyone, doesn't look a little different, falser, than that of other paintings, and whether
this may not precisely be because it's the real image of
Elizabeth Siddal—dead. Especially since we know, by way
of a confession he made to his brother, that for two years
he saw the image of his wife every night lying on their bed
as if at the moment of her death.

The idea for *Beata Beatrix* is taken from Dante's *Vita
Nuova*, which speaks of Beatrice's mystic passage to heav-
en. The painting's right-hand side shows the desolate
streets of Florence, with the Ponto Vecchio and the
Duomo in the distance; Dante himself is also there, looking at the Angel of Love on the left. Beatrice is sitting in
a trance beside a sundial which shows that it's nine o'clock

(the time of her death on June 9, 1290), while a bird with a halo places a flower in her half-open hands. The Bird of Annunciation has turned into death's messenger, and the flower is not a white lily, but a poppy, the red flower of passion, a symbol of sleep and the source of opium: the drug that killed Lizzy Siddal. That's what the critics say.

I was, of course, ignorant of all this when I was looking at the painting with Victoria at my side.

"I'm sure Rossetti ill-treated this poor woman, that he beat her, and if he didn't kill her, he certainly drove her to commit suicide."

"Even if he abused her, it doesn't mean the painting's bad," I said, defending him.

"The painting's bad in its own right, and if you like it it's precisely because of its extra-pictorial elements."

"Who do you mean by 'you'?"

"Who do you think I mean...?"

"I know, I know: us common and ignorant people."

"Don't be so spiteful," and she pushed me toward the entrance, catching me by the arm.

While we were at the Tate, we didn't talk about the real reasons behind Victoria's disdain for Rossetti. I found it striking that, otherwise so humble and easygoing, she should feel so much hatred for the painter-poet.

However, I didn't attribute much significance to that then. After all, I had other things to worry about. The most important was that I didn't know how long we'd be together; I was afraid she'd glance at her watch at any moment, like Eugenia used to do, and say it had gotten too late for her.

I even thought about resolving the situation right away by telling her, for instance, that I felt anxious enough to take two vials of valium, because I didn't know whether she would leave in a few minutes, or if she was thinking about having dinner with me, or even a cup of coffee, and that I needed to know in order to relax. This kind of situation is very difficult, since one fears that every word one says or leaves unsaid can influence the future of the relationship, and that even one wrong formulation can spoil it all. But of course one never admits to these things—who knows why. Mercifully, it was she who took the initiative once again.

"If you have time, we can have a beer in my neighborhood," she told me. I had nothing to do until eight, when I was to attend the dinner they had organized at the hotel to wind up the conference. Nevertheless, I told her that I was completely free and at her disposal.

We took the tube at Pimlico, changing at Victoria. "That's me," she joked. It's not easy to catch people's eye on the London underground, because the passengers, apart from being used to seeing people from all over the world, tend, for some reason I can't fathom, to gaze at some fixed point straight ahead of them. Victoria, however, was noticed. At least that's how it seemed to me: her elegance, her beauty, even her voice attracted everybody's attention.

What she called "her neighborhood" was South Kensington, of course. She told me she was staying at a small hotel there because a friend, the manager of Christie's, lived nearby. She didn't say whether her friend was a man or a woman, and I didn't ask. She said South Kensington was London's French neighborhood, not as pretentious as Chelsea, cheaper, quieter and a bit more bohemian.

Unfortunately I offered to carry the bag with the books for her. I say unfortunately because this brought up the subject of Dante Gabriel Rossetti again. She told me

that since I was *that* interested in the subject, she could
lend me the books for a few days, and I replied that I'd be
very grateful if she told me something about Rossetti,
since, judging by how much she hated him, he must have
been an interesting character.

She asked me several times whether I really didn't
know anything about him, as if she wanted to make sure
I wasn't pulling her leg, and when I finally convinced her
that Rossetti was simply a brand of shoes to me, she told
me the basic facts: Gabriel Charles Dante Rossetti was the
son of an Italian refugee, a literature teacher who had spe-
cialized in Dante's work. An artist and poet, Rossetti
founded the Pre-Raphaelites and *The Germ*, the literary
periodical that became the main means of expression for
the movement, or "The Pre-Raphaelite Brotherhood," as
it was called. They agreed on several guidelines to follow
in their paintings, which they signed with the group's
acronym, PRB, and this gave rise to several ironic inter-
pretations at the time. A popular one in Rossetti's case was
"Penis is Rather Better."

Rossetti's brother and sister, William Michael and
Christina—the latter being an outstanding poet, or at
least one Virginia Woolf liked—also wrote for *The Germ*.
The Pre-Raphaelites represented the culmination of a
process that had begun with romanticism, whereby the
model came to be considered the artist's equal.

Perhaps Victoria didn't tell me all this on that occasion; maybe I read it in one of the books she would later
give me as a present. Anyway, the fact is that in 1850 Rossetti met Elizabeth Siddal, or Lizzy, a beautiful red-haired
woman of twenty-one who had previously worked in a hat
store. She became the Pre-Raphaelites' most beloved

model. She appears in several of Rossetti's paintings, and was the source of inspiration for many of his poems.

They married in 1860. It's said that Rossetti mistreated her and repeatedly cheated on her with his other models. One year later, in 1861, Siddal had a miscarriage, a tragic event which worsened her already weak health. She died the following year of a laudanum overdose. Her death was held to be an accident for some time, but apparently she left a suicide note which was spirited away by one of Rossetti's friends. Full of grief and repentance for the way he had treated his wife, Rossetti buried the only copy of all his poems with her. In fact, Victoria was right in saying that Rossetti was more of an illustrator than a creator, for even the tragic act of putting poems in a coffin at a funeral had been thought up by his sister Christina more than ten years earlier.

We must assume that Rossetti thought highly of his poems and never got over losing them. The feeling that his romantic act resulted in a great loss for literature must have grown stronger in him with time. It isn't difficult to imagine him undertaking the impossible task of rewriting them, obsessed by their loss, incapable of writing new lines.

However, it's said that his friends, in particular the painter and poet William Bell Scott, convinced him to recover the work he had buried with his wife, and, seven years after her death, Siddal's body was disinterred. Rossetti, who by that time was living with Jane Burden, herself a model and the wife of William Morris, another Pre-Raphaelite painter, was not present when the body was exhumed. According to the legend, when the grave was opened on an October night in 1869, "the radiant brightness of her red-gold hair blazed forth from the grave with all the splendour of life... that golden hair undimmed in death."

Victoria told me the essentials of the story in a pub in Onslow Square, surrounded by young men dressed in the customary blue, gray and pinstriped suits. They had just finished work, had dropped their briefcases on the floor and were laughing loudly, holding pints. Naturally I found the story impressive, but not as frightening as she did. But frightening isn't the right word. As I said, she found Rossetti's behavior utterly repulsive; the way he had offered his poems to his dead wife as a token of his love and then taken them from her again seemed extremely mean to her. That's why she hated him and disdained all the Pre-Raphaelites.

"I can't understand that kind of attachment to one's own work. The obsession with recovering your own little verses."

I'm sure she used the word obsession. I didn't defend Rossetti (it didn't even occur to me) though I understood his behavior, at least to some extent. I understood the initial impulse, which showed his generosity, and even better the subsequent regret, the obsession with the buried poems. I told her that to some degree I did understand his wish to recover the lost lines. I said it because I didn't want her to think I was one of those obliging men who ended up agreeing with everything she said.

We each drank two pints of beer. Victoria said she normally didn't drink alcohol. "I only drink when I'm feeling good." After the second one, you could tell she was feeling happy. I was also happy, euphoric to tell the truth, that she'd said she only drank when she felt content. We—well, she—kept talking about art. She said that, much as it saddened her to admit it, there were many mean artists. I remember it well, because her taking such a dim view of some of the artists she knew made me feel happy, inasmuch I wasn't counted among them.

I told her it couldn't be all that bad, that there are base people in all professions, but she didn't listen. She even wondered aloud whether one didn't in fact have to be somewhat base to be an artist.

"Artists subordinate everything to their work. There's nothing more important to them, and those with any success are generally tyrants who try from their youth to convince everybody around them that the most important thing in the world is what they do to a canvas or a stone."

She rested her folded arms on the table, leaned forward and looked straight at me, her eyes sparkling. I was certain that she liked me, that she felt at ease with me, and that the beer had intensified her feelings. I felt the same.

She shook her head as though trying to dispel her gloomy thoughts, but only started all over again. When she talked about the baseness of artists, she seemed to be speaking from personal experience. I wavered between asking her and staying silent, but finally did ask what she based her low opinion of artists on. She stretched out her arms to indicate that, "*hélas,*" she had too much evidence. But aside from personal experience, she had always found it amazing that the retrospective exhibitions of the greatest artists should include their earliest works: sketches of hands and nude torsos, the kinds of clumsy attempts we've all made, and which the rest of us would have lost or thrown away, but which they, the great artists, keep with jealous zeal, convinced of the importance they will some day acquire, not because of their objective artistic value, but simply by virtue of being created by a genius.

While she talked she kept playing with the beer drops the glass had left on the table, a warm, slightly sad smile on her lips. Of course there was also the ability of famous artists to turn anything they signed into gold. Sedano used to call the psychological effects this ability could have on some artists—Picasso was an example—the Midas Syndrome. I seized the chance to tell her that I was working with Sedano on the *Creative Madness* project, because it makes a better impression than simply being the author of *Landscape and Gastronomy*.

"Picasso," she said, "though he was the greatest, should have thrown away three-quarters of his work. He was stingy, like most of them. But of course nobody has yet matched your friend Rossetti."

"Why do you call him my friend?"

I myself was surprised by the way the question came out: I said it with a stutter, like a child who's been punished with no dessert. I could have told her that I had lost a novel, and that, though it probably wasn't much worse than any other, I wasn't too worried about it, because I believed that once you've cleared the hurdle of your first novel, you can write many others. I didn't get the chance, though, because Victoria put her hand on my forearm and leaned a little farther across the table. "I'm just talking for sake of talking, only joking," she explained tenderly. "You don't look stingy." And her sweetly sad smile enchanted me.

"A samba without sadness is like a wine that doesn't make you drunk," I remembered, and ventured to say, "*Une femme qui ne serait que belle.*"

"Meaning?" she said playfully, and took her hand away.

"I don't know why, but the film just came to mind."

"You find me deeply inspiring, then."

"It wasn't a bad film."

"I saw it not long ago and it hasn't aged well at all."

"Don't be so harsh, we all age."

She fell silent for a long time, gazing at me. I didn't dare say anything. In the end, she asked me if I was free for dinner. I told her I was.

"I usually dine at a friend's house, but I'll call her and tell her not to take the cucumber out of the fridge. Because that's all she does." She talked while rummaging for something in her big bag. "Cucumber sandwiches every night, and smoked salmon now and then, also with cucumber."

She asked me to lend her some coins to call her friend from Christie's. "How does the saying go…" she said, holding her hand out to me, "nobody's ever invaded the English, because if they did, they'd have to eat their food."

"Well, we did invade them."

"We? Who's we?" she said in amazement.

"We Bardulians."

"I don't believe you."

"Ask around High Rochester. There is an inscription on Hadrian's Wall where the first cohort of Bardulians offers the building to the mother goddesses. It's the only instance in the Roman Legions where the offering is made in the name of the whole troop and not just the officers."

"My mother didn't know that. She always told me that we Basques were a peaceful people who had only fought for our freedom." She got up from the table and held her hand out to me, palm up. "You're a fine one: I ask you for some coins for the phone, and you hit me with that!"

The opportunity to display a hint of erudition had made me forget her request. I apologized, emptied my pockets and put all my coins in her hand. "All right, all right, I don't want to buy British Telecom," she said, taking two coins and giving the rest back to me. I thought I ought to call Sedano to tell him I wouldn't be there for the end of the conference, but then decided the best thing would be to leave a message at the hotel, because I was sure that if I spoke to him he would make me feel bad about not going. He was an expert at making people feel guilty. But I had to leave some kind of message so he didn't think anything had happened to me. I therefore got up to make a call too.

The phone box was between the ladies' and men's toilets and Victoria was holding its door open with her back, probably because she was about to hang up. "OK then, see you later. Kisses." I heard her say when I came close. She made a kissing sound and hung up. She smiled at me, but not like before. It was a nervous smile. Maybe she was annoyed that I had walked up to her while she was talking.

"Sorry," I told her, "I have to leave a message myself."

"Sure," she said, and gave me back one of the coins I had lent her.

After shutting the door, and as I was dialing the number of the hotel, it struck me that she might have been talking to a man. That was the negative thought. The positive thought was that I didn't have to worry about having listened while she was talking—after all, she was the one who'd held the door open. That showed it hadn't been a private conversation, and that she didn't care who heard it.

The hotel receptionist didn't understand me when I told him I wanted to leave a message for Sedano; English people don't understand English very well. They put me through to his room, and I heard Sedano himself at the other end of the line saying, "Hello. Hello." I had to hang up, of course, and even though I felt like a traitor, I overcame my scruples and phoned again, making it clear this time that I only wanted to leave a message. I would not be there for dinner. "Room 207, no dinner."

When I walked over to our table again I had almost forgotten my dark thoughts: I say almost, because they never abandon us completely. In any case, Victoria's attitude that evening gave me no reason to think she had a man waiting for her somewhere.

She took me to an Italian restaurant. It was called Cesare's or Riccardo's, I don't remember which, and I don't even know why I'm mixing the two names up. It was close to her hotel, on a parallel street, Fulham Road, I think. The owner, Cesare or Riccardo, was a young man, tall and thin, with a sad-looking face, pale skin and dark hair. He looked like a romantic artist. He gave Victoria a warm hug, but without the verbosity these kinds of men often show. No "*cara mia*," and all that. He simply pulled her into his arms without saying a word. As a result, there was a kind of imbalance between the warmth of his embrace and his silence which made the former seem excessive. Perhaps that was the very effect he had been aiming at: emphasizing the gesture of the embrace. When she finally disentangled herself from his long arms, Victoria told him she wanted a special dinner that night, and that he had better concentrate because she was in the company of a Basque, and she had told him how sybaritic we Basques were about food.

"Yes, of course." They would do their best, as they always did when they had the pleasure of her company.

They'd pull out all the stops, as she deserved. And admittedly the food in that restaurant is excellent, even if I can't remember its name. While we ate we rehearsed the cliché about Basques and good food. I did most of the talking, since it's a topic I'm a near-expert on. After all, I haven't been working for two years on *Landscape and Gastronomy* in vain. Flaubert's *Dictionary of Received Ideas* defines "Basques" as "the people who run best." Today, it should say "the people who eat best." In fact there's a Spanish translation that says this.* I don't know whether it's on purpose or by mistake, but it updates Flaubert's cliché appropriately. More than that of other countries, our cuisine depends on raw ingredients from land and sea. The best chefs agree that hake in parsley sauce is one of the most delicious dishes in the world. Besides, it's easy to prepare. There's only one problem: our hake, the principal ingredient, is being fished out, and, gastronomically, African hake in green sauce is about as interesting as a margherita pizza. Fortunately, the younger chefs are making great efforts to create a more elaborate cuisine, rooted in tradition but open to the rest of the world, and not as dependent on scarce ingredients.

It's a cultural metaphor, of course, but I don't know if she got that.

She didn't know much about the subject, and I got the impression that she was listening carefully. She seemed amused that I was well informed in areas that didn't interest her much. She didn't know, for example, that most of the hake we eat comes from Argentina or Chile, at best, or

---

* In Spanish, "correr" (to run) and "comer" (to eat) are very similar. Hence the confusion between "the people who run best," and "the people who eat best." (T.N.)

else from Africa. And like many other people, she thought that if we believe the fish of our coasts to be better, it's only because its trip from the sea to our plates is shorter, and probably also because we're biased, not because fish of the same species that live in different waters are "essentially different," as she added mischievously.

She was wrong, and I had to explain why. The belief that our fish is the best is no myth; it has a scientific basis. It's all to do with the plankton. Our continental plate is short and narrow, but it has tropical flora and the water is cold. These two opposing factors give rise to a special kind of plankton that in turn produces the best fish in the world. Not for much longer, though, for the best species are dying out.

"So the Hondarribia hake isn't from Hondarribia," she said sadly.

"And the sea bream from Orio isn't really from Orio, nor are the elvers from Aginaga really from Aginaga. Not to mention the famous 'fresh' sardines of Santurtzi. And artichokes from Tudela usually aren't from Tudela, but from Murcia, and more often than not canned."

"Don't go on, please. I'd rather not know."

My digression on Basque cuisine was too long and, what's worse, overenthusiastic. I even made a drawing to show her how to distinguish between our hake and the South African one: ours has a bigger head, the others have longer mouths. Thinking back, there's no doubt that, from the point of view of the financial institution that funded the project, I had spent too much time on *Landscape and Gastronomy*, echoing tired clichés and shutting my eyes to the fraud of our cuisine.

The fact that I had admitted to her from the beginning what my real job as a writer consisted in made me feel more comfortable. Nevertheless, I also told her that I was writing a novel, though this wasn't completely true. I was intending to write one but hadn't begun yet.

"I'm working on a novel at the moment," I told her, and, with the posture she adopted when something aroused her interest—folding her arms and leaning over the table—asked me what it was about. As I have often found myself in this situation, I instinctively explained to her that talking about literary works in progress brings bad luck, and she didn't insist.

When we had finished our coffee, Cesare or Riccardo offered us a liqueur, but we'd already had a glass of *vin santo* with some pastry, so declined his offer. Then we argued about who should pay the bill. Due to my many complexes, I insisted too vehemently on paying, though she was the one who had invited me for dinner. I still flush with embarrassment as I remember it now, for I talked so loudly that everyone around us could hear me. I said things like, "No, no way," and, "What would people say?" Finally, the Italian settled the issue: he took the bill, tore it up and put it in his pocket.

That took me aback. In fact it left me paralyzed. I mumbled again that I wanted to pay, but Victoria pushed me, softly but with a firmness that left no room for argument, toward the exit. She told me in a low voice to leave it, that she would sort it out with him another day. The man said, "*Ciao, cara.*" To her, not me.

As we walked away, I told her, out of pure resentment, that Rossetti must have looked like him, and that made her realize she'd forgotten the books about the Pre-Raphaelites in the restaurant. We had just turned around to go back when we saw Cesare or Riccardo bounding toward us with the bag in his hand. "*Il pasto spirituale,*" he said, holding the bag in the air, not knowing whom to give it to. Victoria took it.

"How embarrassing," she told me when he had gone back. "He'll think I'm interested in the Pre-Raphaelites!" I don't know if she intended it as a joke, but I tried to defend them once again, though my arguments were thin. Knowing that late-nineteenth-century painting is considered more luminous than that of the early part of the century, I ventured to suggest that they had a very good command of light, and I must have been right, for she admitted that they used special techniques to make their paintings more luminous. Luminosity, she explained, is achieved by applying white pigment on the canvas and painting over it while it's still fresh. But she added that, in any case, even that was not invented by the Pre-Raphaelites.

We were walking slowly and seemingly without aim. At least I had none, though I suspected we were heading toward her hotel. As often happens to couples wandering without purpose, we walked apart, so that many passersby came between us, interrupting our conversation. The streets were bustling, and the benches outside the pubs full of young people. South Kensington is a lively area, but nice, since it's not as crowded as other places, like Covent Garden, where all the tourists go.

"How nice South Kensington is!" I said.

"It is, isn't it?" she replied, her gaze fixed on the ground, as if she were looking for something on the sidewalk. "Those late-nineteenth-century painters didn't use art as a means of exploring life, like Novalis, Stendhal, Goya or Turner, but to escape from it."

She said it very slowly, as if painfully recalling a text she had learned by heart, and then fell silent, I suppose because she felt she had expressed her thoughts accurately.

I felt sorry for the Pre-Raphaelites, and for myself. I'm not sure I can explain this. Often when we feel sorry for someone, it's only a cover for self-pity. The way Victoria in her bright way projected onto me all the things she hated about the Pre-Raphaelites was upsetting me. She held out the books, and I fancied she could read my mind: "What I find really disgusting is having to deal with these dirty old men who use art to feed their morbid eroticism. And perhaps the Pre-Raphaelites aren't to be blamed for that."

"No, of course not." That was precisely what I had meant all along.

"Nevertheless, your friend Rossetti…".

She stopped in the middle of the street, and I searched her face for a sign of whether she was teasing me again.

"My friend…"

"Your friend, yes. How could he hold his poetry in such regard that he could have someone retrieve it from Siddal's corpse? How miserly! He didn't have the generosity of spirit to give them up for lost, or the talent to create new and better ones."

I don't know why, but she seemed to be putting the blame on me again. It seemed like it was me she despised, as if I were responsible for the impulse to open the tomb and take back the poems. No doubt something I had said had made her think I was capable of such a thing, and I therefore took the tactical decision to distance myself from Rossetti and the rest of the Pre-Raphaelites. I wouldn't defend them again, not even to show that I had an independent mind.

I told her that, come to think about it, I agreed with her that Rossetti's behavior, his need to recover the poems, was somewhat suspect, for the true poet contains within himself an endless wellspring of inspiration. I resolved to tell her about my lost novel and even regretted not having told her about it before, while we were sitting at the table in a quieter and more comfortable place. If I had had her in front of me I would have been able to modify my story, adding or omitting details according to the expression on her face. Our current situation, walking through the crowds on Old Brompton Road, wasn't exactly ideal for storytelling.

I told her the basics: that I'd lost a novel, the outcome of several years' work, which I was quite proud of. Of course I didn't tell her about the German girl who didn't shave her legs. "You see," I told her, "I started to write a new one right away; I didn't even think about re-writing it." Maybe I went too far. I told her I couldn't even remember what it was about, and added that in fact I didn't care, because my sources of inspiration were inexhaustible.

"I hope you'll let me read the new one when you finish it."

"Sure."

I hoped to have made it clear that I wasn't like Rossetti.

We were already at the foot of the steps leading to her hotel. It was an ordinary house with two floors and an attic. Its front porch was framed by two white columns. Its name was a number: 169, perhaps, I'm not sure. It was the same as the street number. Victoria told me someone had set a crime novel in that hotel. Its title was the same: *Hotel 169*—or maybe it was 196. She confessed she hadn't read it. "The one you'll write though, that one I'll read."

She was standing on the first step with one elbow on the banister. Her posture seemed to suggest she wanted to part as soon as possible, especially because she had one foot on the second step, ready to go up. I thus had ample evidence to believe that she would say goodnight at any moment and disappear forever, though I had to admit that the languid way she leaned on the banister might also indicate a willingness to keep talking to me.

If this second hypothesis were true, however, it would require an appropriate topic of conversation, an interesting or funny subject that would satisfy her, for women usually enjoy laughing more than anything; they want us to be fun to be around. I knew all that, but couldn't come up with anything interesting or amusing to say. All I could think about was my own paralysis. In that moment of despair, I even wished she would say "Goodbye" and go away. Anything seemed better than standing there at the foot of the stairs, struck down by an anxiety that brought me out in a cold sweat.

I counted to ten to clear my mind. Naturally it's often useful to count higher, in order to thrust away anxious thoughts; but at that moment, standing in front of Victoria, I didn't have time for more. Sedano, being an analyst, isn't fond of these behaviorist tricks, but I think that, though they may not solve the problem definitively, they do bring some relief, at least sometimes.

On this occasion, however, it didn't help me think of anything interesting, least of all witty. For some reason I kept thinking about the Pre-Raphaelites. One of them, Millais, I think, reminded me of Klimt, the Viennese artist who was said to have a golden touch for painting women. Such things crossed my mind. I even thought up a comment I could make on that subject: "The Pre-Raphaelites already had Klimt's golden touch," or something in that vein, but in the end I didn't say it, because I thought it might be merely rhetorical rather than genuinely interesting. Besides, I might have risked being told she wasn't interested in Klimt either. I didn't ask her, but I'm sure she isn't.

That's how things usually happen. But now I'd like to know even that, I mean whether she likes Klimt or not, and I would ask her without worrying about whether it was interesting or witty. And without being afraid to bring up the Pre-Raphaelites again, I would repeat to her what William Morris used to say to his wife Jane, who was later to become Rossetti's lover: "I cannot paint you, but I love you."

Rossetti did paint Jane Morris, however, and did it well. After all, women usually end up with men who paint them well, not with those who love them best. Meanwhile I felt unable to utter a single suitable word, and Victoria didn't say anything either. She looked at me, with a playful smile I thought, as though it amused her to be the cause of my ineptitude. Finally deciding not to bring up Klimt, I looked at the sky for help, and seeing no other way out, told her that at least we had been lucky with the weather.

She agreed and looked up too. The moon seemed to glide smoothly on a strand of clouds. "Let's see if it holds out tomorrow, in the morning at least."

We stood looking at each other. I also hoped the weather would stay good until noon, because I had to take a plane in the morning. I didn't need to ask why she only cared about the morning weather: "I have mornings off," she said. "I have to be at Christie's in the afternoon, so the rest of the day's weather doesn't really matter." After a short pause she asked, "Do you have any plans for tomorrow morning?"

I had booked a flight for seven o'clock in the morning, but of course I told her I was free.

"We could go for a walk then if you want."

"Great!"

Suddenly, knowing that I had the entire morning to be with her, the acute anxiety I had felt in thinking that the future of our relationship lay in the balance disappeared. I had another morning: eternity. I felt the way death row inmates must feel when they're pardoned at the last minute. Now that I had been given until the following noon, I realized the proper thing to do would be to take my leave, but somehow I stayed there, undecided about returning to my hotel and unable to utter a word. Until she said, "I'm terribly tired, and I guess you want to go out with your friends. I'm sure you've got something planned."

I wasn't sure how to interpret her words. Was she simply sending me away for being a bore, or was she really so tired that she thought I might prefer to be with Sedano, listening to jokes about neurotics, rather than standing beside her under the moon?

"I'm tired, too," I told her.

Still, we lingered there indefinitely, she on the first step and I on the sidewalk, mouthing empty words to fill the silence.

"Well..." She finally bent down from her heights and offered me her cheek, so that I had to raise mine to her like a schoolchild. She was wearing a very subtle perfume that I hadn't noticed until then, and though her kiss was a matter of pure civility, I felt I had caught a glimpse of her private self. It was a thrilling feeling.

After having exchanged the inevitable and pointless phrases ("Whenever you want," "No, no, you decide," "I don't care"), we finally decided that I would pick her up at her hotel at nine o'clock, and that afterward we would simply walk around London.

When I got to my hotel, the first thing I did was look for Sedano, but, conveniently, he wasn't there. I sat down at the desk in my room and wrote him a message: I had received a call from my publisher telling me to go to a London publishing house, which had offered to publish *Landscape and Gastronomy* provided it was rewritten and set in Scotland. I had a meeting at nine o'clock to discuss their terms, so would postpone my return to Bilbao.

It was a preposterous story, but I didn't care. The point was to let him know that I wouldn't be traveling back with him so he didn't have to worry about looking for me. Then, maybe because the ease with which I had written the note raised my spirits, and because I was at my desk, pen in hand, I decided to take advantage of that moment of inspiration and write a few lines to Victoria too.

I sat there for a long time, at the kind of desk that seems to be made for writing suicide notes, unable to write a single word. Or rather, I did write one word, only one: "Victoria." I collected my main ideas: "You seem unreal, a dream," "I'm the happiest man in the world because I've met you," "I'd rather die than never see you again." But I was unable to form a paragraph that linked them.

It was four in the morning, and I was still sitting at the desk trying to write a sentence that would encapsulate my feelings, when Sedano knocked on the door. He asked me what the hell this was, holding out the note I had left for him at the reception, and I repeated what I had written, adding that it might be the opportunity of a lifetime. He was drunk and had to catch a plane at seven, so I got rid of him quite easily. But he warned me that they wouldn't change my flight or give me my money back. I didn't care; I told him again and with more emphasis that it was a once-in-a-lifetime opportunity, and pushed him into the corridor. Then I copied my main ideas into my notebook: "You don't seem real, you're like a dream, so beautiful," "I'd rather die than never see you again," "I'm the happiest man in the world because I've met you."

The following day we headed north on foot. We had arranged to meet after breakfast, but I didn't have time. In fact, I didn't have time for anything; I'd only fallen asleep after Sedano had left for the airport because he had knocked on my door again as he was leaving, to remind me that I'd lose the money I'd spent on my plane ticket. Psychoanalysts tend to worry more about money than they think they do.

Just in case, I asked Victoria if she'd already eaten breakfast. Sadly she had, and for a while we talked about the buffet breakfast fraud: how they charge exorbitant prices for a few slices of buttered toast and how, on top of that, you have to put up with the stink of sausages and eggs fried in fat. But the truth was that I could have eaten anything at that moment. I didn't feel very well.

Victoria, on the other hand, looked refreshed. Her hair was still wet from her shower and she was in a very talkative mood. She made interesting and witty comments about everything she saw; at least that was my impression. Everything around us suggested something to her. She made me see a lot of things I wouldn't otherwise have noticed, and I felt I was seeing many things for the first time, with new eyes. Trees, for example: I learned to distinguish between the severe ones, the melancholy ones, the noble, the base, the proud or faithful, even the misanthropic. On the way, we stopped to talk to a group of old men who had greeted Victoria. It was clear that she enjoyed their attention and that she liked the old rascals

too. The squirrels were familiar with them and answered
their calls, jumping down from the trees and up onto their
hands. This gained our genuine admiration, which in turn
made the old men puff up, and they started to compete
among themselves, making the squirrels jump in more
and more spectacular ways. Then they put a few hazelnuts
in Victoria's hand so she could feed them too.

I can still see her, kneeling on the grass and calling out
to the squirrels, surrounded by the old men, who whistled
at them. They asked her what we called them in our language. "*Kattagorri*," she said, looking at me to make sure
she was saying it right. "Category," said the old men
laughing. She explained to them that the squirrels in our
forests are red, not gray like the ones in London, but that
you hardly see any these days. "You're very nice, like a category."

We crossed Marylebone Road and entered Regent's
Park. I didn't ask her where we were heading. We didn't
seem to have any clear aim. She praised the gardens, and
this reminded me of the day I spent in the Botanical Gardens with Eugenia. Victoria asked me what I was thinking
about. "Oh, nothing," I said. She said she didn't believe
me, and added that she'd been thinking how good she felt
just walking around London, so good she was actually
conscious of it. She laughed. I tried to tell her I felt the
same, but she interrupted me again.

"You know what? I've changed my plans," she told
me. "I have to go to Paris tomorrow, but to make up for
it I got out of a dinner engagement I had tonight."

I bitterly regretted having told her the previous day
that I would leave in the afternoon on the first plane to
Bilbao. "What a shame you're leaving," she said. "If you'd
been here we could've had dinner together again." She

seemed genuinely sorry, and maybe that was what provoked my knee-jerk reaction. I told her I'd changed my plans too.

I said it without considering what excuse I would make up to explain my change of plans. Anyway, lying wasn't a big problem for me anymore. I told her I did have to go and that I had intended to take that plane, but that, unfortunately, I hadn't been able to get a ticket.

That was the first thing that sprang to mind.

"I'm sorry," she said. "But only a little," she added, laughing.

I wasted the opportunity to tell her something nice, for instance that I wasn't sorry at all. Indeed, I was glad, not just because I'd have another chance to dine with Victoria, but also because I hadn't actually booked my ticket yet and therefore wouldn't lose my money a second time.

"I wouldn't have thought that so many people traveled to Bilbao on a normal weekday."

Her doubts didn't worry me. As a last resort I could always tell her that the hotel receptionist had given me wrong information.

"Neither would I." I told her that it might be because of the new Guggenheim Museum in Bilbao.

"Let's see how long it lasts." The world had gone crazy—a few idiots go somewhere and everybody follows them. Anyway, she was sorry I had had to give up my plans. Did it cause me much trouble?

"No, I don't mind much." Actually, I said, it was all right, since I also liked walking around London with nothing to do. That was as close to my true feelings as I dared come. I didn't have the courage to admit that, though I had already checked out of the hotel, I would readily have slept on the street just to be able to dine with her, and even to spend another minute by her side. But I may not have been completely aware of my feelings at the time.

"Anyway, that means you're free for dinner."

"Yeah," I answered, not too enthusiastically.

"Great!" she said, obviously pleased.

Naturally I was a bit worried about the logistics of it all. I had already checked out of my room, and my suitcase, which I was to pick up in the afternoon, was already at the reception desk. I was afraid that when I returned I wouldn't be able to get another room.

The street we were walking along had veered uphill and was now lined with terraced houses.

"We've gone off the map," I said.

"Adventure is adventure," she replied without stopping.

She didn't seem to know where we were going. She added: "You don't seem like much of an adventure-lover, though."

"Not much, no," I had to admit.

"Of course—you writers go for inner adventure." She was laughing at me now.

"Don't laugh, there's something to that."

"No, I'm not laughing," she replied holding back her laughter and vigorously shaking her head.

We were face to face, and she put one hand on my chest in that gesture that's usually intended to stop the other person from getting closer. I didn't move. "I'm serious," she said, doing up the top button of my jacket. "I'd like to write too, but I have to make do with reading."

She said that one of the things she liked most was when she was about to begin a new book by an author she loved. Setting up the right environment, collecting the things she would need: tissues, a pencil, the teapot… "But these are very intimate things, and I don't want to open the doors of my private life to you," she warned me. Still, I knew what she was talking about. Anticipating the pleasure of the journey. Music? Well, that couldn't be planned ahead. Usually no music, for each piece of writing has to create its own. I asked her what she liked to read, as Eugenia used to ask me. Everything. She seemed to be an eclectic reader. She was familiar with some writers who are usually considered difficult, but at the same time she wasn't ashamed to show that she had gaps which would have been considered inexcusable in some intellectual circles. She didn't keep abreast of new publications, and when she found a book she liked, she read all of that author's works.

On the few occasions when she had found a book difficult or boring, but had gone on reading it because of the admiration she felt for the author's other work, she had never regretted it. She quoted Claude Mauriac's words: "The reader's effort and, having made this effort, his pleasure." I could have replied, "O tempora! O mores!" which are important words, to be taken seriously. But usually she was quite merciless: whenever she came across a book she didn't enjoy, she would stop reading it.

We had been walking up a lonely, moss-lined lane for a considerable time, now and then coming across a Victorian or Georgian house. Passing a group of houses in the Tudor style, I wondered whether they were genuine or recent imitations.

In Britain, even new things, especially when they're made of wood or red brick, don't need much time to wear and acquire a noble air of antiquity. I suppose it's the climate. My doubts were therefore reasonable, but she assured me the houses were new. "When you're in London it's easy to imagine that the slab you're walking on or the banister you're touching have been trodden on or caressed by Dickens, or Woolf, or Rossetti."

Laughing, she leaned against the mossy trunk of a chestnut tree. They were both beautiful: the huge chestnut tree glowing with green and the laughing Victoria, barely real in the cold light that surrounded her.

"Maybe your friend Rossetti wrote a poem sitting on that bench." She pointed at one of the wooden benches you find in any London park. I was about to warn her that she would stain her clothes on the moss, but stayed silent. I didn't want her to move.

"Why 'my friend Rossetti'?" I asked her again, but she didn't answer. Maybe she hadn't heard the question; she was deeply engrossed in what she was saying: the magic of those cities where you felt the presence of the past, which had a culture of making things last. Not a bit like ours, where we threw everything away without compassion. At home, for instance, you couldn't walk on the same pavement your grandfather had walked on, or touch the same banister, because we changed them nearly every year. It was a culture of poverty. Poor people renovated their kitchens more often than rich people, because rich people made things to last. Because we couldn't afford good things, we aimed for new ones instead.

"Don't you think so?"

The park was dressed in its finest early autumn gown. The luxuriant trees, crowned with gold and fire, still showed no signs of decay, and some of them, like the one supporting Victoria, proudly kept their verdure alive. I told her she was right: poor people's houses were always being repaired and never looked beautiful. For a while I wondered whether to ask her again why she kept saying "your friend Rossetti," but in the end I didn't. I warned her that the chestnut tree would stain her jacket, and she moved away. She didn't bother to check if it was dirty.

After moving away from the tree and having a look around, she said, "I think we're in Camden," and we started to walk again.

We didn't find anyone to help us in the park, and lingered at a crossroads near the exit not knowing which direction to take. It must have been obvious that we were lost, for a man in a dark formal suit approached us to offer his help. He asked if we were looking for Karl Marx's grave and we both said yes at the same time. After all, the man assumed the most natural thing to do in that area was to look for Marx's grave, and we didn't want to disappoint him.

He gave us precise directions and following them we soon came to the top of a hillock from which we could see the black iron gate of Highgate cemetery. The gate was slightly open, to permit one person to enter at a time.

An elderly, typically English woman appeared holding a typically English collecting tin (the kind that resembles a pitcher of beer) and clearing her voice asked us for a pound each to visit Marx's mausoleum. It's a rather ugly building a few feet from the entrance at Highgate East.

After seeing it, we crossed the road to the gate at the opposite end. It was firmly shut. That part of the cemetery has a more mysterious air, perhaps because the tombs are hidden behind the walls of a building that resembles a gothic cathedral. As before, a woman appeared, again typically English: short white ponytail, bright socks, and a voice that sounded like door hinges in need of oil. She told us that, as the guided tour was about to begin, we could join in. And again, we didn't dare reject her offer.

We paid for our tickets, and when she asked for an additional fee that would allow us to take pictures, told her we didn't have a camera. We then joined the group, which included six other people. All were elderly, except for a woman in her thirties. The guide was a big strong man in his forties who looked more like a football coach than a cemetery guide.

At the archway of the main entrance, he explained that he was a member of a charity, the Friends of Highgate Cemetery, a voluntary association that had taken charge of restoring and maintaining the cemetery, which had been abandoned until about twenty years earlier. I feel sorry now that, at the time, I wasn't aware of being in the most interesting necropolis in Britain, but in my defense it was hard to imagine, given its deplorable state. The weeds had overtaken the stone to the point of completely covering the tombstones, some of which were broken or displaced, as if a band of body snatchers had been on the loose. Many of the crosses lay on the ground and the memorial statues were crippled, missing arms and legs. The cemetery was consecrated in 1839, but it looked five hundred years old.

We had just set off on the tour when it began to rain, but the people in our group didn't open their umbrellas; they carried on impassively along the gravel path. And since worrying about getting wet seemed quite out of place, we lingered at the rear of the group so we could open ours, though we felt a little embarrassed about it.

The young woman in the group had an American accent and seemed to be a regular visitor, because she talked to the guide as if she had known him all her life. I thought she might be writing a doctoral thesis on some topic related to cemeteries, but Victoria said she looked

like a necromaniac. "If I weren't here she'd rape you on a
tombstone, I'm sure." I felt a bit embarrassed by Victoria
mentioning sex, even though she'd intended it as a joke
and had said it in a very natural way. "See? She's looking
at you," she said. And so she was: gazing at me, laughing,
displaying two rows of big healthy teeth. A few moments
later she approached me and asked me to take a picture of
her sitting on Michael Faraday's grave.

I don't remember all the celebrities who are buried in
Highgate, but the guide mentioned a long list of very rich
people; he also said it was a very expensive cemetery. He
mentioned Christina Rossetti, Dante Gabriel Rossetti's
sister, and, of course, Elizabeth Siddal: Beata Beatrix, Rossetti's model and wife.

When he mentioned Siddal, however, he informed us
that we couldn't visit her grave. It was in a completely
inaccessible place, surrounded by dense bramble and,
what was worse, impossible to get to without stepping on
a number of other tombstones. There was a general
resigned sigh. These people had come to the cemetery
specifically to see Siddal's tomb, and they were obviously
disappointed. "If you want, we can sneak away and look
for it on our own," Victoria whispered in my ear. "You
can't leave without visiting your muse." I smiled at her.
Apparently the school-trip atmosphere of the tour
(indeed, the guide was looking at us very severely, calling
for our attention) was giving Victoria an itch to break the
rules. We would soon discover, however, that the guide's
comment had had no other aim than to make visiting Siddal's tomb more desirable, and to increase our excitement
when he later told us that we would, after all, be able to
see it. Indeed, a few moments later the guide raised his
arm, asked for silence—"Attention, please"—and informed

us that today he would make an exception: he would take us to see Siddal's grave, albeit briefly. A delighted murmur rose from the group, and when the guide said, "Follow me," they all ran after him. So did we, of course, though it wasn't an easy path. In fact, there was no path: there was a dense overgrowth and a lot of mud, and the tombstones, which the guide had entreated us to respect, and which we mercilessly stomped on, were extremely slippery.

We finally arrived at the Rossetti family vaults. The people in our group, who until that moment had behaved politely, started to push to get as close to the crypts as possible. I didn't see much, mainly because Victoria stood apart from the group, and I didn't want to show too much interest in Siddal's grave and give her the impression that I was as ghoulish as the others. Besides, just as the guide was informing us that the tour would continue in two minutes' time, the American woman came over and asked me to take another picture of her. She sat on the edge of the tombstone and said, "Cheese." Then: "Another one, please."

As I was trying to get her into focus, Victoria, who was standing behind me, said, "Well, I'll leave you two alone." The American woman reclined on the tombstone at full length. I had barely pushed the button when she again commanded, "Another one." This time she pulled her skirt up to her waist, laughing. I gave her back the camera as soon as I had taken the picture; I didn't want to continue with that game, and besides, I could no longer see or hear the group.

I'm not ashamed to admit that I felt uncomfortable and frightened. The place looked like it hadn't been visited by a Christian soul for centuries and, though some of the graves were quite new (I had read on the tombstone that one Harold Ford Rossetti had been buried there in 1982) and many tourists like ourselves visited it every day, it gave one the impression that the tombstones might start moving at any time and the bodies emerge from their graves, Elizabeth Siddal among them, with her long red hair and the Bird of Annunciation and the flower of passion in her hands. Suddenly terrified, I got out of the place by jumping from stone to stone, while I heard the laughter of the American woman behind me. I kept running through the bramble until I caught up with the group. They were walking in line; Victoria was last.

"Where did you leave the toothy necromaniac?" she asked.

"I don't know, I ran for my life."

She came strolling along about thirty feet behind us, unconcerned. Indeed, the rest of the group's curiosity also seemed to have been sated by Siddal's grave, and they didn't listen as attentively to the guide's explanations as before. There was no escape, though. We had to visit yet more sepulchers of various famous people I hadn't heard of. At length we reached the Egyptian avenue, a road lined with heavy iron gates guarding the crypts, which the guide said had recently been restored. However, this so-called restoration had respected the rust, mold and spider webs; or who knows, perhaps Victoria was right and it was a result of the British talent for restoration, for making new things look old.

According to the guide, the Egyptian avenue narrows slightly toward the end, to create the illusion that it's longer than it is, and ends in an archway with obelisks at both sides: a reference to the Valley of Kings. Near to it is the Circle of Lebanon, a kind of round island with long crypts, which Victoria and I passed over, as did the American girl, who was following us at some distance. The Circle of Lebanon is crowned by a beautiful cedar tree, one of whose branches had been broken by the wind some days before. "A terrible loss," said the guide.

There was a table with books and postcards by the exit. "We've got some new material," we heard the guide say to the American woman, confirming to us that she was a regular visitor. We didn't stop to buy anything. The American bid me farewell me with a drawn-out "Byee." Victoria walked away quickly and I hurried after her. I didn't want her to think I was interested in cemeteries or Rossetti, as indeed I'm not.

Fortunately the rain stopped. We followed the same road that had brought us to the cemetery, because though we had first wanted to take the same road back, we decided it would be easier to find some form of transport farther ahead, as we already knew there was nothing for a considerable distance behind us. "We'd need a taxi now," Victoria said, and then we both fell silent, perhaps because we were walking rather fast.

At length we got to a crossroads where we saw a taxi parked beside a phone box, and someone who could have been the driver speaking on the phone. We waited for him to finish, and having made sure that he was the driver, Victoria asked him if he could take us to the center. The center of where? He didn't seem to be joking, so we told him it was the center of London we wanted to go to.

We decided that Victoria would get off at the Cromwell Road and Queen's Gate junction and that I would continue to my hotel. Then we would meet at about eight outside her hotel.

When I got to my hotel, the first thing I did was book my ticket for the following day. British Airways had plenty of vacant seats on its evening flight. I then tried to take a room in the same hotel for one more night, but this time I was unlucky; it was full. They could, however, find a place for me in a similar hotel in the area if I wished.

I suddenly remembered that, around the corner from where Victoria was staying, there was another hotel of the same type, called *Switzerland* or *Swiss*, I wasn't sure. I asked them if they could try there. Though they finally consented, they did so reluctantly, probably because they considered it inferior. In any case, there was a vacant room at the *Switzerland*, or *Swiss*, so I picked up my luggage, asked for a taxi and set off for South Kensington.

I chose the hotel to be as close to Victoria as possible, of course, though I was running the risk of being seen by her and being caught in a lie. Nevertheless, making up an excuse, just in case, wasn't difficult for me. I decided to tell her that, though in the morning they had promised me that I could stay one more night, when I came back in the afternoon I was told there had been a mistake ("Can you believe it?" I would add) and that there were no spare rooms. I would also tell her that, since I didn't care where I stayed, and as we had arranged to dine at Cesare's or Riccardo's, or whatever the restaurant is called, I had decided to find a place in her neighborhood.

The implausibility of my excuse didn't worry me in the least; after all, I didn't mind her guessing my true reasons for staying at the hotel next to hers. Nor did I worry that she would find out I had already postponed my flight twice just to be able to dine with her. I even think I hoped she would find out for herself what I didn't dare say. Obviously—how clearly I see it now!—it would have been better if I had dared to do it myself; if, instead of lying, I had told her, "I had intended go back this afternoon, but I'll stay if it means I can have dinner with you tonight."

It seems so easy now, but at the time I was convinced that her having invited me to dinner twice didn't give me the right to think that she felt anything special for me. The invitation, I thought, had been issued only because we happened to be two strangers in London who came from the same city and had nothing else to do, and in that context it didn't have much meaning; it was like small-talk in waiting rooms or on trains. To admit that I had stayed only to be with her would have been like trying to shape destiny. I might have put her in an embarrassing situation and even risked losing the chance to dine with her that evening.

So I stayed in my room the whole afternoon, just in case. My window gave onto one of those dark alleys below street level where the garbage bins are kept, so that I could only see the legs of the people passing by. Also, though it led to Old Brompton Road, it did so in the opposite direction from the underground station, making it quite unlikely that Victoria would walk by.

Until about six in the afternoon, I kept myself busy writing a kind of epilogue for the next edition of *Landscape and Gastronomy*, in which I explained my thesis about our cuisine: the need to adapt its traditional features to changing circumstances, precisely to avoid losing them. For purely environmental reasons, the classic Basque dishes have a very uncertain future, at least those that require substantial raw ingredients from our soil or sea. Production being so small-scale, ingredients are scarce and expensive. From the point of view of their availability, our elvers, hake and squid are becoming delicacies, like caviar. They can be the inspiration or even the essence of a dish, but not their only ingredients. We have to welcome new products and fusion cooking, but without forgetting our main challenge: to protect the regional varieties of plants and fish, which are fundamental to our cuisine, and which are dying out due to inadequate policies and resources.

It was more or less the same cultural metaphor Victoria had found so interesting when I had told her about it the day before, but the financial body that funded the project would probably reject it for being too critical. After all, they only wanted me to fill in the gaps left on the pages between photographs, which presented an idealized image of a vanishing world (the cherished homestead, the picturesque fishing boat, the clay pot with a typical dish) with suitably purple passages. I therefore knew my text was useless, but nevertheless I felt quite relieved, having for once written what I thought.

I switched on the television, but there was nothing interesting on, except a commercial for a pornographic film they were showing on one of those cable channels that only let you see a few seconds of the film unless you pay. And I didn't pay, of course. I kept pressing the button every thirty seconds—to see the image for about three seconds at a time. Basically, it was the same shot all the time: a huge penis and a mouth sucking it. I spent half an hour in front of the screen, watching about three minutes of

the film in total, until I got bored, or restless, and went to
the window to look outside.

Whenever a beautiful pair of legs walked by, I would
convince myself that they might be Victoria's. But even
that exercise was making me terribly nervous, and in the
end I had no alternative but to go out and buy some cigarettes, for even though I had given up smoking long
before, they helped me control my nerves.

This relapse into the habit of smoking, as well as
being shut up in that small room with its sad furniture for
such a long time, depressed me terribly. However, this was
exactly the kind of situation I had found inspiring in former times, especially when I wrote poetry, so I sat down
in front of a sheet of paper again. Victoria had told me
she'd like to read something I'd written. Actually, everybody says that when you tell them you're a writer, but
then again I hardly sold three hundred copies of *Farewell,
Sadness* in my day.

As I said, I was in the best possible mood for writing,
but the words wouldn't come. I could only write, "Victoria, because of you I've started smoking again." I thought
about adding something like, "I can't live without you; I
need you by my side forever," but I couldn't bring myself
to put it on paper. I was totally blocked, mainly because I
suspected Victoria wasn't very fond of excess; she liked
balance and moderation. The paintings she had admired
at the Tate gave me that impression, because she had told
me she liked Brancusi and Matisse and sometimes found
Picasso excessive.

Many attempts later, that sentence—"Victoria,
because of you I've started smoking again"—remained the
only line on the paper, and I entered a new phase where,
coming to the window again, I didn't even have to con-

vince myself to believe that every woman who went by
was Victoria. I therefore had to run out several times and
check before they turned the corner, until I had to stop,
because the receptionist, his four oily hairs in a pony tail,
was scowling at me, I guess because I was distracting him
from watching television, which was all he ever did.

After that second phase, I entered another, in which,
incapable of doing anything else, I lay on the bed,
restraining myself from smoking and going to the window, and trying to come up with something more literary
to add to "Victoria" than, "because of you I've started
smoking again." In the end I fell asleep, and when I woke
up, not having time for a shower, I changed my shirt and
dabbed some cologne on my neck. Plenty of it. Too much,
perhaps, for as I hurried past the reception desk I noticed
the receptionist flaring his nostrils and sniffing the air.
Naturally this didn't do much to boost my confidence.

As I turned the corner and headed for Victoria's hotel,
she was already standing outside waiting for me, dressed
all in white, smiling broadly, her hair still wet from the
shower she had obviously had time to take. As I hurried
toward her, she politely told me, "I've just come down,"
without giving me time to excuse myself. She didn't seem
surprised that I hadn't appeared from the direction of the
underground station.

We went directly to Cesare's, or Riccardo's. To my sat-
isfaction, the owner didn't appear when we entered. I
ordered the *capelletti* stuffed with pheasant, the same dish
that Victoria had eaten the previous night, and it was delicious. With the dish in front of me, however, I couldn't
avoid returning to my theory about ingredients. I worked
out that it couldn't contain more than a third of an ounce
of pheasant; the rest was butter, flour and a few plain veg-

etables. That was the strength of Italian cuisine. "I've been writing about that this afternoon," I told her, without realizing that I'd talked about the same thing the night before.

"And did you do anything else?"

Gastronomy didn't seem to interest her much. However, she looked at me very attentively, in that posture of hers: arms folded on the table, leaning slightly forward, smiling. I didn't know what to say, so I resorted to the same old excuse—that I had scribbled a few lines for the novel, but that I didn't like to talk about unfinished work.

"Then tell me something about the ones you've finished."

It wasn't worth it. In fact, I felt embarrassed even to mention its title. Indeed it was the title that embarrassed me most, so explicitly did it reveal my source of inspiration. I had chosen the title as a homage to Sagan (I had been about to call it *Nauseous*, which would have been even worse) and have bitterly regretted it since, because in fact *Farewell, Sadness* is not the act of plagiarism its title suggests. But of course it was a foolish mistake, and one that gave the conceited critics an undreamed-of opportunity to unleash all their venom without much effort, especially as I was a young writer who was only starting out.

I was thus about to keep the title of the novel from her with the excuse that I had forgotten it myself, but this didn't seem plausible, so to cut it short I told her that my first novel, *Farewell, Sadness*, had been the product of my salad days, and that it had no real value. As for the second one, I had lost it in Paris, as I had already told her, and I had had to make a great effort to forget about it, since I didn't want to write the same novel again.

She asked me why. Apart from being impossible, I answered, it was tedious. Each time I had to answer that question I did it with more confidence and flair. "What the wind sweeps away is no more. It isn't the worst imaginable fate for literature." I knew she wanted to hear that I wasn't the kind of sterile poet who cries over the memory of a lost line. "After all," I said, "the spring in our hearts never runs dry."

She liked it, of course. "See?" she said. "That shows a generosity of spirit quite unlike Rossetti's." Her eyes sparkled at me over her wineglass. "To unearth a corpse just to get back a few paltry poems! Because that's another thing—the poems weren't worth a damn."

Once again I had the impression that, with Victoria, it was possible to hold opposing views. Not that she was the kind of person who gave in easily to avoid conflict; she listened carefully to my arguments. At least that was my impression. And that's important, since, for a civilized discussion to take place, each dialectic adversary must display at least a semblance of interest in his opponent's arguments. If discussions end up in fights, it's usually because we don't listen to one another. When one listens attentively, tiredness or boredom are the only risks, never anger.

Besides, Victoria was good-humored enough to turn the conversation around completely when she felt we were taking a topic too seriously. But when we touched on the subject of Rossetti things were quite different. Then she would become serious, quite unshakeable. "Let's leave that one, shall we?" she said, leaning toward me again. "Come on, tell me something about your writing."

I don't know why—I must have been drunk—but I told her that the best thing I had ever written was a text of about ten lines, which I had sent to a woman I wanted to seduce. I had been after her for a long time, but she hadn't paid the slightest attention to me. Until, that is, I sent her that short note. When she read it, she fell madly in love with me. Or perhaps with the text, I wasn't sure.

"How interesting!"

She really did seem interested. Her eyes brightened and she leaned forward even more. So much so that I instinctively sat back. She was the very image of curiosity, and I felt enormous pleasure at having aroused her interest with my own words. For a moment I even thought that the story of my sending the note to Eugenia could be made into a novel.

"How interesting!" she repeated, but sadly she didn't have time to say more, because at that point the owner came to our table to greet us. After the usual exchange of compliments, Victoria introduced me with the words, "My friend here is a writer." I don't know why. Perhaps what I had told her about the seductiveness of my text had stuck in her mind. Or maybe she was just excusing herself for having dinner with me a second time. He told me, in Italian, that I was very lucky. Apparently, he didn't think I could possibly understand English. "*Che fortuna! Il dono de la parola giusta.*" Something like that. Then, putting a hand on Victoria's shoulder, "*La parola giusta per sedurre una donna.*"

I told him that wasn't a bad way of defining literature—ironically, of course, for I thought Victoria must have realized how corny he was. But I don't think she even heard my comment. They started asking each other about their mutual acquaintances—other clients of the restaurant, I supposed—in what seemed an endless conversation to me.

As they talked I thought about Eugenia, about how brave I had been to send her the note and about the effect it had had on her. It had been a restrained pluckiness, it's true, for I had hidden behind my literary intent. As for its effect, I had never been so aware of it as when I was telling the story to Victoria, so I tried to recall the words that had had the power to make Eugenia love me.

I couldn't. "You'll be lying on a bed, naked"; "the pearls of water on the bottle"; "the fire burning in your thighs." I couldn't connect the bits I remembered. I didn't even remember how the text began, and of course it was impossible to pull it together with these scraps. I could hardly believe I had forgotten so important a text, given its impact. I was at once trying to remember the text and puzzling over my inability to remember it; and of course, pondering two things at the same time doesn't help much. However, that's precisely what we often do: in addition to trying to recall what we've forgotten, we compound our worry by thinking it's on the tip of our tongue, that we're losing our memory, growing old, and so on. This explains why, often, as soon as we forget that we've forgotten something, it comes to mind by itself.

The best thing would therefore be not to think. Fortunately, the owner pulled me out my whirlwind of thought. He was asking me if I'd like an amaretto. Victoria suggested that we accept, since it was our last night in London. After that, however, we didn't stay long, because we both had to get up early the next morning. She had to take the train to Paris.

We didn't fight over the bill as on the previous night; she let me pay. Having bid the owner goodbye, we went outside. We were very close to her hotel, but spontaneously took a stroll around the square to make the time last a little longer. As we walked, the bay windows of the houses we passed let us gaze into the comfort of their bourgeois interiors: living-room crannies bathed in cool amber light, richly furnished with paintings and well-fitted bookcases, perfect for a quiet talk.

The atmosphere in the street was also pleasant. It wasn't raining, and though it was wet, it wasn't cold; the wind blew just enough to whip up the dry leaves from the ground.

"*Les feuilles mortes,*" she said smiling. "Those three words are enough to evoke my entire literary and emotional life," she told me when I asked her why she was smiling. "That's the gift of writers, particularly poets—that's what Riccardo was talking about." She said Riccardo, not Cesare. She stopped just ahead of me. "You don't like Riccardo."

"You know," I answered, "every handsome guy is an enemy, at least potentially."

"He paints," she said without laughing at my joke. "But I shouldn't think he's very talented." Then, after a short pause, as if she regretted her harsh judgment, she added that she didn't know why she would think he was bad either, since she hadn't seen any of his paintings; he didn't hang them in the restaurant, though, and that must mean something. "Don't you think so?" she asked.

I told her I did, though I didn't know in what sense, good or bad. I didn't want to keep talking about the guy.

"It's true," she said pensively. "On the one hand it could be a sign of modesty, but it could also be the opposite: he's too proud to show his paintings in a restaurant."

She seemed to realize that the subject didn't interest me, and fell silent for a long while. Probably we were both engaged in the difficult task of finding something else to talk about.

"You will at least agree with him on one thing," she said, leaning toward me again. "Literature is the gift of seduction."

"*Il dono de la parola giusta per sedurre una donna,* that's what he said. The art of finding the G-spot, if I'm not mistaken."

"Don't be nasty."

She said it because I was making fun of the Italian, of course, but it struck me, though I was probably wrong, that she might also be chiding me for bringing up sex.

"You yourself have admitted that you seduced a woman using literature."

We had left the peaceful square and were on Old Brompton Road again, but here it wasn't too busy either. She stopped one or two steps ahead of me, in that peculiar way she had: she would overtake me and then stand in my way facing me while she talked. "You can't deny that."

I could have told her I was just joking, but I wanted to continue the game. While I searched for an appropriate answer, I played for time by telling her I didn't remember.

"You remember, of course you do!"

"All right, I admit it. After all, it's impossible to write without being aware of one's own power of seduction. That might sound pretentious, but it's true." I put my hands in my pockets to avoid any ostentatious gesturing. "I admit that a dozen of the lines I've written have had the power to make a woman mad about me."

"A dozen."

She said it as if the number was what struck her most. I didn't know whether she thought it was too many or too few.

"A dozen lines, yes, and they too were swept away by the wind," I added, perhaps because I'd been unable to remember them.

"You lost them, too."

"I sent them to a woman, and of course didn't keep a copy for myself."

I wasn't in the habit of keeping copies of my own letters for posterity. I had hoped she would understand this without my having to say it.

"So you'll have to open Siddal's grave to get them back." She laughed. "I hope you'll do it with your own hands, rather than sending someone else to do the job, like that rogue."

"That's just what I'll do," I laughed back at her.

We kept walking, slowly, as though not wanting to reach our destination, but at the same time not talking much, aware that we'd get there sooner or later.

We didn't have time to start a new conversation. "It's like when your ship is about to set sail," I thought to myself. "You close your book, pick up your things and get ready to go aboard." Moreover, the few words we said to each other were about leaving. She said she had to get up early—which didn't make it easier for me to suggest that we have one last drink. She had a lot of work to do, and was leaving for Paris in the early afternoon.

"While I'm flying to Paris, you'll be on your way to Bilbao," she said. I'm not sure what she meant. Perhaps only that.

I asked her if she would be staying in Paris for long, and even thought of telling her that, by the way, I had to go there myself, and that it would be great to meet again. She said she'd stay there for three or four days, then go to Madrid. Where did I stay when I went to Madrid? Eugenia leapt back into my mind.

Victoria didn't like the Chamartín hotel either. Women like small old hotels. Men prefer large modern ones, probably because they provide the necessary discretion in case the opportunity for an affair presents itself, a possibility they never quite dismiss.

She usually stayed at a hotel, of course. It was on Serrano Street, at the very top end, one of those little palaces that abound around El Viso. Her errands in Madrid would take a week, and she hoped to be able to spend some days with her mother afterwards.

Although we couldn't have walked more slowly, we eventually arrived at her hotel, stopping at the foot of the steps. It seemed to me that she was allowing time for something that couldn't come. It was the kind of situation where you say, "Well…" and, "So…" and then fall silent again. Once at the door, she said, "Well…" twice, and I had the impression that her eyes were encouraging me to ask if I could come in with her; but she also mentioned that she had to get up early in the morning, and that's not exactly what a woman says when she wants to spend the night with you. I resolved not to rush things, but leave them as they were. After all, sooner or later I would have the infallible formula to spark the flame of her love. I only had to write a dozen powerful lines.

At length we said goodbye. Her cheeks were cold, but a delicious warmth seemed to emanate from her body. "I've had a very good time, honestly," she told me, breaking my heart in pieces. I felt my eyes tear up.

The following day I didn't emerge from my room until it was time to vacate it. It wasn't because I had woken up late—I had watched an Indian man opening the corner shop as the last night owls tumbled home with slow, hesitant steps. I saw waves of passing legs coming and going, in and out of the underground station. And finally, at midday, that corner of South Kensington looked very much like a quiet neighborhood in a provincial town.

I didn't identify Victoria's legs, nor any that might have been hers, and therefore didn't feel the excitement of uncertainty, of having to run out of the hotel to see if it was really her. At noon, before leaving my room, I called Eugenia for the first time in two long years.

I'm not sure I knew why I was calling her. A secretary at her office told me she wasn't feeling well and had taken the day off. I remembered that I had her home number, which until then I had never thought of using. I decided to try it, hoping her husband was at work. I was wrong. A man's voice answered the phone, and after he had said, "*Dígame?*" three or four times in an increasingly angry voice, I simply hung up. He had a gruff voice, the voice of a man with a hairy back.

It was past noon when I installed myself at a Café Rouge, one of those cafés that strike you as uniquely Parisian the first time you see them, until you realize they're part of a chain and that there are hundreds of them in London, all of them identical. Nevertheless, it was strategically located to enable me to keep an eye on the entrance to Hotel 196, or 169, or whatever it was called. I drank half a dozen cups of tea, hiding inside the café, and at about two in the afternoon went to sit outside and ordered some apple pie.

If Victoria appeared she would probably see me, especially if she came from the underground station, but I didn't care. I decided that if she saw me I'd tell her I had nothing better to do before leaving. "I'd rather take advantage of the slightest opportunity to see you than go look at the Tower of London," I'd tell her. And if we didn't meet I'd go to the airport and kill time in the duty-free store.

She showed up at four, in a black car that looked like a cab. I mean that it was a large and unusually high car, but it wasn't a cab. She emerged from the back before the driver could open the door for her, and quickly mounted the four or five steps to the hotel. A few moments later a man well into his sixties got out of the car. He had that authentic English look: tall and thin, short white hair, pale gray suit.

He stood beside the car smoking a cigarette. He smoked in that affected way some snobs have of holding their cigarettes away from their bodies. After about ten minutes Victoria reemerged carrying a small suitcase. As the driver took care of the luggage, the man opened the door for her and got in after her. Then the car pulled away and quickly disappeared in the same direction it had come, though u-turns were illegal on that street. Several cars honked their horns and, beside me, the waiter of the Café Rouge said, "Crazy man!"

"Crazy!" I agreed. I paid my bill, tore up several sheets of paper on which I had written, "Dear Victoria" and a few other silly things, and headed for the underground.

On the plane back to San Sebastián, I persuaded myself that I would overcome my obsession with Victoria as soon as I settled back into my daily routine, but it was not to be. On the contrary, it got worse. I spent my days trying to write to her, trying to worm out from my memory the dozen lines that, as Riccardo had said, would help me seduce Victoria. And that wasn't the worst of it: for professional reasons, I had to eat out too many times, and everybody knows it's virtually impossible to eat healthy food in Basque restaurants. The vegetables, for instance, apart from being canned most of the time, are also as dangerous as oxtail, because the chefs have persuaded themselves that they have to sauté them in butter, with plenty of garlic and bacon. I therefore had an upset stomach most of the time, which only increased my melancholy.

I spent my days waiting for the night to come, so I could go to bed and lie in the dark thinking about Victoria. My intellectual activity during the day consisted mainly in coming up with narratives for my nightly fantasies—I did practically nothing else. I tried to eat dinner early so I could go to bed as soon as possible. Then I usually imagined myself writing a short note to her. A dozen powerful lines on thick paper, which I would send to her Paris address: "You'll be lying on your bed, amid silken sheets, your thighs burning, and I'll come in holding a cold bottle of champagne." I would put together the bits I remembered from the note I had sent to Eugenia, and add whatever my Muse inspired. This wasn't a great deal, since for some time I'd been incapable of writing anything but rubbish, and even though I occasionally managed to finish the twelve lines, and once or twice even went so far as to switch on the light and commit them to paper, when I looked at them again the following day, I always found them hopeless and threw them away.

In my fantasies, however, the note invariably filled Victoria with intense emotion. She'd call me a couple of days later, telling me I was incorrigible: "*Tu es un coquin.*" She would also say that my words were like lips caressing her skin, her mouth, her eyelids, that she felt their heat climbing up her thighs—things like that. I'd have her say, "I'm in Paris," or London, or farther away, because increasing the distance, physical or temporal, increased the pleasure of my longing. The call could come from anywhere in the world, but she unfailingly told me, "I'll be in Madrid the day after tomorrow," at the small hotel on Serrano Street, and always at seven. "I'll be waiting for you at seven o'clock." This was probably because I had gotten used to calling it a day by that time.

Over the following days I tried to get in touch with Eugenia several times. I never got ahold of her at her office, and when they asked me if I wanted to leave a message, I refused to give my name. When I called her at home, it was always somebody else who picked up the phone: a woman, whom I thought was probably the housekeeper, or the hairy-backed man, and at least two different children. When one of the children picked up the phone, I felt terrible, like a criminal breaking the peace of a home. In any case, as soon as I heard, "*Quién llama?*" which was what the hairy-backed man usually said when he answered the phone, I quickly hung up without saying anything.

In the end I had to admit that I was only searching for Eugenia because I wanted to recover the note I had sent her two years earlier. Once I had admitted this, I decided that I would pursue this goal until I achieved it. I picked up the phone and dialed her number. I heard the voice of the woman who might have been the housekeeper on the other end, but this time I left a message for Eugenia, saying who I was and that I needed to talk to her—though I still didn't know what I would tell her.

She answered my call within the hour, catching me unawares. I hadn't yet thought of a good excuse for calling her again after two long years. I told her I wasn't calling her for any special reason, but that I often thought about her and had decided to give her a call on the spur of the moment.

"I really shouldn't speak to you. You really screwed me over." She told me I'd hurt her a lot, and that she'd gone through some tough times because of me. She repeated several times that she'd felt awful. I told her I was sorry, that at the time I hadn't realized how much harm I was doing her. To be honest, I couldn't understand that my departure could have caused her so much suffering.

"You think I'm the kind of woman who sleeps with the first man she sees?"

I told her that of course I didn't think that, and that I didn't take just anyone to bed either. For a moment I thought of teasing her a bit by saying, "They have to meet the minimum standard!" but thought better of it, put on an earnest voice, and repeated what I had said before: that it had also been very important to me, and that this was precisely the reason why I had run away. I hoped she would understand.

And she did understand. "I must be stupid, but I'm actually touched you called." And then, just as the woman was describing an emotion that was quite incomprehensible to me, I had a revelation: I was incapable of making love to anybody but Victoria. I wished I had somebody to share this feeling with, for I did feel real emotion at the thought that, sometime in the future, I'd have another chance to be with her.

"Don't exaggerate," I told Eugenia, half jokingly. To tell the truth, her cloying sentimentality was unsettling me.

"It's true. I really want to see you."

I said I felt the same and took the opportunity to add, as casually as possible, that I had to go to Madrid in a few days' time and that I hoped we could meet.

She asked me to call her without fail. How happy she was. Really impatient to see me. But then she returned to the same old theme: how badly I had treated her and what a horrible time she had gone through because of me. In the end I had to tell her I had a lot of work to do.

"What are you working on?" she asked.

I talked to her about *Landscape and Gastronomy*. Well, in fact I only mentioned it. I also said that I had just returned from a conference on literature and psychology, and had started working on a new novel there. "By the way," I told her in a moment of inspiration, choosing my words carefully, "it's turning out a bit too erotic."

"Erotic?"

I can't say for sure whether she said it in happiness, confusion, or disbelief. I had thought it would be a good way to bring the conversation around to the subject of the note. The idea had entered my mind in a flash. As somebody said, inspiration usually finds us at work. However, I cunningly refrained from letting the cat out of the bag too soon. I had to avoid arousing her suspicion.

"And you, what are you doing?" I asked her. She was working on an important corruption case; I must have heard about it in the media. ("What planet are you living on?" she used to ask me whenever I revealed my ignorance of something I should have known from the papers.) She was overburdened with work. It was the most important challenge of her career, and it didn't leave her time to read, go to the cinema or listen to music.

Nevertheless, she recommended a book by a young writer which she called "absolutely indispensable," and a couple of films I hadn't even heard of, which of course prompted her to say, "What planet have you been living on?" Then, returning to her old ways, she offered an analysis of Arzalluz's latest imbecilic utterance, and asked me what was wrong with us Basques, without really asking, for she gave me no time to reply. I wanted to tell her to get lost and leave me alone, but didn't—for Victoria's sake, of course, and because I was determined to achieve my objective.

To this end I went to the bookshop the following day, bought the book by the young writer that Eugenia had recommended and learned the blurb on the back by heart. Then I went to the library and found the review it had received in *El País*, which, needless to say, called it "indispensable reading." In the following two days I also saw the two films she had told me about.

I called her three days later to tell her how much I had enjoyed them all, to ask her to recommend another book or film, and to complain that that I didn't have much spare time, mainly because of my damned novel.

"Oh! Your erotic novel."

I felt the excitement of a fisherman when he feels the fish nibbling at the bait before it swallows it. I told her that my novel's erotic tone was entirely her fault. When I thought about her I wrote things that surprised even myself, indecencies that otherwise didn't suit my nature at all. Inevitably, she asked me to elaborate. Finding myself with no other alternative, I had to tell her the first thing that crossed my mind: smearing her with jam from head to toe "and that kind of obscenity." Not too original, I must admit, but she didn't seem to be looking for originality. Her voice deepened at the other end of the line and she said, "I'm dying to see you," carefully pronouncing each word. I quickly made up an excuse and ended the conversation there, before things cooled down.

We talked on the phone every day, at least twice a day, and I didn't find it hard to maintain her interest; she seemed very receptive. And since she seemed quite taken by the jam idea (she often asked me, "Tell me, what part of my body are you going to rub?" as soon as she picked up the phone), we mostly stuck to that topic.

Paradoxically, the jam idea, which had been so important in restoring our relationship, was to almost undo all the progress I had made until then. The problem arose because the fictional representation didn't take into account the inconveniences involved in actually carrying out such a scene. Such as staining the bedclothes. And since several details made me suspect that she had been in this kind of situation before, it suddenly occurred to me to ask her what we'd do with the sheets. It made me flush with embarrassment to think that we'd have to leave them with strawberry stains, or wet, if we tried to clean them. What if the hotel staff sent the police after us? All this entered my thoughts, but I only said, "What about the sheets?"

I won't reproduce here the scolding she gave me, because luckily it had no serious consequences. She first fell silent, as if she hadn't heard me, then said, "What do you mean, 'what about the sheets?'" When I answered, "You know, the stains," trying to be as concise as possible, she seemed to understand everything. And it suddenly dawned on me that I was guilty of a major faux pas.

"The stains. Listen to you!"

I was tied to my mother's apron strings, or rather, to the priests' cassocks, she said. "I pity you," she said, and then, "I pity all of you," directing her anger at all of us Basques. We had been brainwashed by religion and nationalism. And religion and nationalism were the same thing. "The same shit."

"You're right. The same shit."

Fortunately I had quick reactions, and unlike on other occasions, I told her she was right. After all, wasn't nationalism just another form of religion? I was completely fed up with politics, "With the politics at home." When I realized my statement had calmed her down a bit ("No wonder," she said softly), I decided to stop pussyfooting and get to the point. After all, I had been on the verge of giving it all away by proceeding too slowly.

I told her I was screwed. Whatever they may say, women can't hear that statement without being moved. I was screwed, I was suffering from writer's block, among many other things. Then, as if it had just occurred to me (which, to some extent, it had), I told her that in my novel the protagonist sends a note to the woman he loves to try to win her over, and that I had thought of using the same note I had once sent her, as a tribute to her. Did she know what I was talking about? Maybe she had forgotten.

"Are you crazy? It's the most beautiful thing I've read in my life." She always carried it with her. Did I want her to read it to me?

"If you want to…"

"Hold on."

She put down the receiver. Not for long, though. Before I had time to count to twenty, I heard her voice say, "Are you there?" and I sharpened my senses like a goalkeeper waiting for a penalty, ready to copy the text word for word. But when she started to read, she did it so well, with such panache, that I couldn't pick the words out one by one; I got carried away by the text. They were only words, plain words: hand, bottle, tongue, water, beads, but her honeyed voice made them sound sensual, almost steamy, so that they were no longer words but caresses, each and every one of them. When she stopped reading and said, "How wonderful" ("Not bad," I admitted), I hardly thought the words were mine, so good did they sound. However, I only remembered the same elements as before: her lying on a bed, naked, on silk sheets if I'm not mistaken, me entering the room with a bottle of champagne, the beads of water on the cold bottle, and the heat between her thighs.

I didn't care much at first, it's true, because the joy of finding the text good overshadowed any other feeling. I was certain that, if I had wanted her to, she would have read it to me as many times as I wished. I could have asked for it right then, pretending that hearing my words read out in her silky voice excited me. In my madness, it didn't occur to me that the text was completely irrelevant, and that, read in her sexy voice, anything—St. Paul's epistle to the Corinthians, say—would have sounded equally sensual and arousing. At the time, I believed her passion was purely a product of my text, and naturally this increased both my sense of its importance and my determination to retrieve it.

After that last telephone call, I was sure that I would get that damned note back before long and without too much effort. It was partly for this reason—because I considered myself already in possession of that weapon—that I felt bold enough to call Victoria in Paris, in order to test the water. I thought carefully about whether to call her at home or at work. If I called her at home I'd be taking a step toward intimacy by behaving like a friend. This might be too daring. But if, on the other hand, she wasn't upset by my calling her at home, I would know she considered me a friend.

However, prudence was a virtue I valued above all others in those days, and that was why I chose to call her at work—if things went wrong, if I suspected that my call annoyed her, I'd have plenty of excuses to preserve my dignity. I could tell her, for instance, that an uncle, a priest, had left me an old painting of St. Augustine, and that I thought she might be able to refer me to an expert who could value it. In fact I wouldn't be lying to her, because I do have a portrait of St. Augustine which my uncle left me, though it clearly isn't worth a cent.

I therefore decided to call her at work, but I was determined not to make up any excuses unless it proved strictly necessary. If she asked me why I was calling, I would simply admit that I wanted to know how she was doing. Besides, I wanted to avoid having to send St. Augustine's painting to a valuer, since I knew it would be a waste of money.

I called her office. I first had to spell out my long Basque surname for a secretary. I then had to talk to two other people before I heard Victoria's clear, cheerful voice. My heart was hammering. When she said, "*Allô*," I replied, "*Hola*," which she then repeated as a question. Obviously she didn't recognize my voice, or, what was worse, my name, though I'd just spent half an hour spelling it out to her colleague.

"You don't remember me," I told her dryly in Basque, preparing to accept my defeat with dignity.

"Oh, Rossetti! Of course I remember you!" she said, almost without giving me time to finish.

At that moment, two thoughts struck me at the same time. On the one hand, it was obvious that she hadn't recognized me until I had spoken to her in Basque, which didn't exactly make me leap for joy, since she probably didn't get many phone calls from Basques. I also had another doubt—was she calling me Rossetti because she didn't remember my name, or, given her opinion of the painter, for another, much less desirable, reason?

"Of course I remember you. Tell me, have you gotten your poems back?" Her voice was jolly.

"You're obviously in high spirits today," I said sharply, and even considered switching to plan B and telling her that I simply wanted to get in touch with someone who could value a painting I owned. But that would have been terribly foolish. She answered that I was right, she felt very happy, because Paris was very beautiful in that season, and above all because she was organizing an exhibition of the work of several Basque artists, which she was very enthusiastic about.

She then asked if I was still writing. She told me she was eager to read something I had written and that, when

my novel came out, she would put it in a suitcase and go
to a house a friend of hers had in Normandy, where she
would have all the time in the world to read it. She wanted to "give it every chance," so that if she disliked it I
wouldn't have a single excuse. Did I approve of Normandy
as a setting for reading my novel?

What else could I say but that I thought it most
appropriate! That I had the damned novel completely
written in my mind and only needed to get rid of my
commitments and get to work. I also explained that at
times I thought the novel was brilliant, that it would be a
success, and at other moments I found it mediocre,
depending on my mood. The kind of thing writers often
say. I must have spoken for too long, because when I finished she asked me why I had called her.

Even though I felt tempted to tell her about the St.
Augustine painting, I finally took my courage in both
hands and said, "I simply wanted to know how you're
doing."

"I'm doing very well, thanks. And you? How are
you?"

"Well. I'm well."

"Oh, that's great, both of us are all right, then!"

She laughed. I didn't know what to say, and we fell
silent for a few seconds. It seemed like an extremely long
time to me. She gave me no indication that she was in a
hurry, or that I was bothering her, but I got the impression that someone else was talking to her, so just in case I
told her, "I'm going to leave you now. I'll call you again
some other day," and she answered, "All right, whenever
you want." Then, after a short pause, she suggested, "Why
don't you come to Paris for a weekend?" and I answered,

"Maybe I will one of these days." "I'll take your word for it," she said and hung up.

I gave much thought to that conversation. I remembered it with absolute accuracy, and sometimes found more reasons to be hopeful about it than other times, depending on my mood. After all, whether you see the bright or dark side of things usually depends on how you look at them. No doubt the negative elements were there. The one I found most worrying was that she hadn't recognized my surname, even if it isn't exactly common, and that she didn't recognize my voice when I said "*hola*"—for I greeted her in Spanish, not Basque. That's what I usually do: I greet in Spanish and then continue the conversation in Basque, as opposed to many who say "*kaixo*" in Basque and everything else in Spanish. And naturally, a brief "*hola*" isn't much help in identifying someone by his voice, especially considering that she would have expected me to greet her in Basque.

As regards my surname, on the other hand, when I managed to look at it in a positive light I thought she might not have forgotten it, but simply might not have been given it. I've seen this happen in many places. They ask for your name by force of habit ("so-and-so's office, who shall I say is calling, please?"), then don't bother giving the name to the person receiving the call, especially when it's long and strange like mine.

Thus even the most negative facts seemed bearable at times, depending on my frame of mind. But of course there were moments when even the most promising ones looked bleak. For instance, there was her suggestion that I come to Paris for a weekend. Rather than being an honest invitation, it might simply have been one of those "*mi casa es tu casa*" expressions we all use—a mere formality

which, since she lived in Paris, she'd have to utter more
often than most people. Not only because Paris is the capital of good manners, but also because its inhabitants are
always being told how lucky they are to live there, and of
course it's nearly impossible not to get into the habit of
saying, "Come and visit whenever you want." Something
similar happens to those of us lucky enough to live in San
Sebastián.

Anyway, I decided not to ascribe too much importance to the conversation, in part because none of the
facts, neither the positive nor the negative ones, were actually very significant. Her calling me Rossetti, for instance,
could be taken as a friendly joke, much as it wounded my
pride at the time. The only important thing was my total
certainty that she'd soon fall madly in love with me, with
the help of the text I was about to recover for her.

The only thing I was hesitant about was whether I
should send Eugenia's text to Victoria as it was or translate
it into Basque. It wasn't an easy question to settle, and the
more I thought about it the more reasons I found both for
and against.

The main argument for leaving the text in Spanish
was that that was the language I had originally composed
it in, and though I was usually very self-critical, I truly
believed the text to be utterly faultless. Even though I
couldn't remember it well, I knew that it was direct, concise and lucid, and had had an enormous effect on Eugenia; of this I was completely sure.

Furthermore, because of her cultural background,
Victoria identified much more with Spanish and French
than Basque (she had demonstrated as much in London
when she had said, "*Les feuilles mortes*"). According to Josu
Zabaleta, the Spanish translator of *Landscape and Gastron-*

omy, the reason why most Basque people find it difficult to read the world classics in Basque is precisely that our cultural background is mostly made up of Spanish texts.

But then there was the emotional effect Basque was sure to have on her. I was certain Basque had a place in her heart. After all, mothers in the Basque Country usually find it almost impossible not to say certain words in Basque to their children, even when the mothers themselves aren't Basque. It therefore seemed reasonable to believe that she must have heard the words "my dear" and "my love" in Basque: *nire maitea, nire laztana*. And since in our culture verbal displays of affection usually end in early childhood, she probably hadn't heard them since then. For that reason it seemed to me that, for once, Basque might not be a bad option, at least for a short and precise text, and in any case there was no doubt that "*te quiero*" and "*je t'aime*" were nothing compared to "*maite zaitut*." I confess I was often tempted to send her those two words and nothing else. Sadly, I didn't. I thought I ought to focus on recovering Eugenia's note first and decide which language to send it in once I had the text.

I don't know how many times I called Eugenia without daring to bring up the matter of the note. But in the process I succeeded in reviving our former relationship; she kept me up to date on the reviews in *Babelia* and fervently praised the books, films and music they praised. She also kept asking what was wrong with us Basques, and I kept telling her I didn't know.

"You're sick," she would say, "you don't realize it, but you're sick."

Actually, I realized perfectly well that we aren't very sound. Nevertheless, it isn't nice to hear an outsider saying it over and over. It made me feel very uncomfortable when I talked to her on the phone. This, and when, having finished commenting on the Basques, she turned lubricious. "You know what I'm wearing?" she used to ask me, and I answered yes or no, whatever took my fancy, because she didn't seem to care. "I'm wearing a pair of stockings and a garter belt. I can slip them off if you want."

She always mentioned the garter belt. Some women think they turn into Mata Hari as soon as they put on a garter belt. I don't know if Eugenia really wore those things or if she was only pretending, but she made me feel extremely uncomfortable. Not that I'm a puritan, but knowing that she was in her office and might be caught doing the things she said she was doing made me terribly anxious.

I sometimes recognized my own words on her lips: "You'll come in with a bottle of champagne in your hands, and I'll be lying on silk sheets, naked." She used to tell me that I wrote like a demon, that my words drove her mad—though in general hers were a lot more explicit. "I'm moistening one finger. Do you know where I'm putting it now?" That sort of talk. I think I had better leave it there.

I decided to put an end to these kinds of scenes. I would call her once more and ask her to read the note again, saying I'd got to the point in the novel where the note appeared, and couldn't continue without it. To do things properly, I bought a device that would allow me to record her voice directly from the phone. The staff in Electroson, the electronics shop where I bought it, gave me precise instructions on how to install it and it seemed easy, but in the end I couldn't make it work. So I had to make do with holding a conventional tape recorder as close to the receiver as possible. And even though this made it necessary for me to hold the phone away from my ear, the system worked well on the few occasions I tried it out.

However, at the very moment when I needed it to work it gave me problems. This in spite of my having tested the method on Sedano before I used it on Eugenia. I called him three or four times, and everything went all right at first. I managed to tape his speech fairly clearly, even though his deep voice wasn't ideal for the purpose. In what I had decided would be my last trial, however, I pressed "play" instead of "record," thus playing part of a conversation I had previously taped. Sedano became suspicious, of course, and, thinking that the Spanish Intelligence Agency was spying on us, came over with one of his clients, an ex-ETA member, to search my house for hidden microphones.

The ETA member—a paranoid alcoholic, Sedano admitted—spent three days in my house with a big pair of headphones on. He found nothing, of course. From that day on Sedano seemed to drink and smoke more, and even lost weight, so worried was he about the whole affair. And since I couldn't tell him the truth—though I would have liked to calm him down—the situation pained me considerably. After all, Sedano is a close friend, and I think he feels the same about me.

Things being as they were, I had to wait another weekend before calling Eugenia again. I called her on a Monday. I'm sure of that, because someone had set fire to the cash machine on my street for the third time the night before, and that usually happened on Sundays. The way some people burn cash machines to protest against the political situation doesn't do *me* any good, because it usually takes the bank a whole month to get a new machine (probably in order to make people aware of the consequences of such vandalism) and I end up having to walk miles to the next branch. The date isn't all that important, I know, but it was a Monday morning. When she picked up the receiver, I immediately realized she was in a bad mood and I remember that I put it down precisely to it being Monday.

After we'd exchanged the usual greetings, she asked me, "Have you heard the news?"

I imagined she was talking about the cash machine on my street. "Yes, it's the third time they've set it on fire," I told her.

"What are you talking about?"

"The cash machine on my street. It's the third time they've burned it. I'm really pissed off."

It was true.

"See? You're totally self-absorbed." It was a phrase she often used, but I didn't understand why she was saying it now.

"What's the matter?" I asked her.

"Two policemen have just been killed a few feet away from here. It's horrible."

"Jesus."

I didn't know what else to say. I suddenly feared that, once again, my plan was foiled, and could only repeat, "Jesus."

"Yes, Jesus. What were you calling me about?"

I don't know how, but I summoned the courage to say, "No, nothing. I just wanted to see how you're doing." I even went much further: "You see, the thing is I need you to read that note again... you remember?"

"Yes, of course. Hold on, I'll go get it."

Finding it didn't take her long. I had hardly switched on the tape recorder when she started to read: "I'll open the door and you'll be lying on silk sheets..." When she had read the first words, however, she started to cry, and I only picked up a few words ("cold bottle of champagne," "pearls of water," "thighs on fire"), probably only because I remembered them from before. I'm not sure what feeling prevailed in me then: surprise at her crying, frustration at once again failing to get what I wanted, or restlessness caused by her sobbing and trying to read the text at the same time. I have to admit that I also felt angry, and somewhat annoyed. I believe crying is a coercive way of expressing one's feelings, since it puts the other person in a difficult position.

"I'm sorry," she said finally, "I can't."

I couldn't understand what was wrong with her, and didn't dare ask, because I knew that one way or another the blame would fall on me. So I asked myself what I had done wrong, while looking at the tape recorder—rolling in vain.

"I can't," she said, sounding calmer already. In fact her voice was quite dry now. "If it's the note you want, you'll have it tomorrow without fail." And she hung up without another word.

I hung up too. I felt relieved at having gotten myself out of that embarrassing situation, and even glad, because success was within reach. But I also felt a bit despondent, and had a slightly upset stomach. Maybe I was more sensitive to crying than I thought.

The following day I received a postcard. It was from Victoria and it depicted a Normandy beach at sunset. The long strip of sand was empty and bathed in the peeled-peach tinge of the sun sinking into the sea. On the back she had written: "*Un paysage merveilleux pour mûrir votre mélancolie. Victoria.*" Nothing else. No best wishes, no kiss, only her name: Victoria.

Naturally, I also gave a lot of thought to this text. The most important, the most heartening thing was that Victoria hadn't forgotten about me. Moreover, though her message was rather cold and laconic, I liked to think that it hinted at my sensitivity. The text was polite and elegant, "*Un paysage merveilleux pour mûrir votre mélancolie*" and, being written in French, it seemed open-ended; because of my linguistic incompetence, *mûrir* looked like *mourir*, so that I sometimes read the word to mean "ripen" and sometimes to "kill" my melancholy. Also, that beach would be a very beautiful place to die in: "*mourir d'aimer.*"

For those of us who celebrate the fall of Babel, this is the true magic of words, of languages: they are precious instruments that reproduce our differing perceptions and sensitivities, and they can sing to us even when we find them incomprehensible. Anyway, for me, those seven words evoked the cozy radiance of a warm sunset, the flavor of ripe fruit and the sweet murmur of the sea. And they filled me with the greatest joy.

It was undeniable that the text was elegant, that it didn't need another jot. Anything added to that perfect sentence, such as "*je t'embrasse*," or "*baisers*," would have spoiled it; the perfect complement was to simply sign it "Victoria."

Sedano agreed with this when I showed him the postcard. I did it out of sheer arrogance—I cannot deny this without telling a lie. I wanted him to know that I had a relationship with a marvelous woman who had written this marvelous line. I wanted to make him jealous, in fact. But I also showed it to him because he's a psychiatrist and I wanted to know his professional opinion.

I didn't have the nerve to tell him that Victoria was the beautiful woman we had admired at the National Theatre. Anyway, I wanted to strengthen my relationship with her before telling him the truth about my London adventure. He didn't say much about the postcard, only that it was written in a delicate, flowing hand by a beautiful and cold woman. But I got the impression that this was only his fantasy, that he wasn't basing his opinion on scientific grounds. When I entreated him to be more specific, to tell me what he thought about her not having written "best wishes" or "love," he first said it was a matter of elegance, just as I had expected, for Sedano isn't stupid; he too saw the sentence was perfectly self-contained.

Intelligence was the second reason, he said (though guessing that I was an immature melancholic wasn't hard, he added with a snort), and, finally, coldness. According to him, this woman wasn't suitable for me.

When I asked him what he based his opinions on, he just said, "Scientific intuition." He was still quite moody after the telephone-tapping affair, and, I think, because smoking three packs of cigarettes a day filled him with remorse, even though he tried to hide it by pretending to be unconcerned, saying that, like Mallarmé, he did it to put some smoke between the world and himself. I couldn't get anything else out of him. His scientific intuition was telling him Victoria was unsuitable for me, that was all.

Naturally I didn't allow his silly remark to overshadow my joy at receiving the postcard. His only problem was envy, and I could already taste the pleasure of introducing Victoria to him. Before long, however, the shadow of another doubt darkened my mind: what was Victoria doing on a Normandy beach?

I knew a friend of hers had a house there, because she had told me she thought it the most appropriate place to read my novel. This was why, even before I received the postcard, I would choose a Normandy beach as the setting for my fantasies—the same beach Victoria could see from her friend's house. She would be reading the final lines of my novel sitting on a chaise longue by the fireplace, and after finishing would remain there with the stack of paper in her lap, staring at the same golden sun I was watching descend into the sea from my own window. Her intense emotion melting into soothing tears, she would sit with both hands on the novel for a long time, even after night had fallen and the last ember in the fireplace had died out.

In the end, she would get up and pick up the phone. At this point I would play Ravel's *Pavana* to create the right atmosphere for the scene. I don't know whether I chose it because it's happy in its sadness, or the other way around. Anyway, the flute posed its question, like a leaf dancing in the air, and just when the violins and violas were about to burst out in reply, just then, my telephone would ring. I would turn from the window: the peal of the call one is waiting for, on which one's life depends, is like a lance to the heart. But I wouldn't rush to pick up the receiver. I would stare at the machine as though it contained the key to the meaning of my life. Eventually, when my need to know finally overcame my fear, I would reach for the receiver, say "Hello" and imagine Victoria's first words:

"This is Victoria."

The clarinets and flutes were tremulous fingers trying to seize the dancing leaf.

"Victoria!"

"I've finished it, and it's wonderful. What can I say: *C'est tellement beau. Tu m'as émue.*"

" . . . "

"I don't have words for every nuance of emotion, like you do."

" . . . "

"The only thing I can tell you is that I love you. Come."

"Where are you?"

"In Normandy."

There were many variants of this conversation, but I always ended up telling her I would leave for Normandy straight away. I would make the journey by car, at night. I don't know why, but it always rained—probably because that's what it's usually like in films. As I tried to keep myself awake at the wheel, filled with an overwhelming joy at the prospect of seeing Victoria, I was usually overtaken by sleep.

Until I started to worry about what she might be doing in Normandy. Obviously she hadn't gone there to read my novel; but that was all I could say with certainty. I didn't even know whether the owner of the house, who might have been with her at that very moment, was a man or a woman, for she had only mentioned a "friend."

At one point I even began lamenting Victoria's sober, elegant style. There was nothing I wanted more than to find one word on the other side of that lonely Norman beach that would at least hint at the answer to all my doubts. I wanted it more than to be able to write down the novel that was in my head. At that moment I would have treasured the kind of ordinary greeting people use on postcards: "I'm here with a group of friends," or, "I've come for an auction"; something that, though it might mar the text's elegance, would assure me she wasn't spending the weekend with the old toff I'd seen outside her hotel.

One thing was clear, however: Victoria hadn't forgotten about me. That was what I repeated to myself again and again by way of encouragement. But at night, when I went to sleep—I still retired early, trying to shorten the days by sleeping a lot—all my efforts to steer my fantasies in the desired direction were totally useless, because although I prepared the scene in detail (the fireplace, the table adorned with flowers and red candles), that man would suddenly appear holding Victoria's hand, and I wouldn't sleep until the finger of dawn closed my burning eyes.

One day I decided to put a definitive end to the situation. A whole week had gone by since I had last called Eugenia, and it was time to ask her to do what she had promised; no more delays. If necessary I would beg her on bended knee. I didn't mind losing my dignity.

I had to call several times before I got to speak with her. Even though she greeted me with a cold, "Oh, it's you. What do you want?" I didn't back off. On the contrary, her rudeness only strengthened my resolve. But simply asking her to return my note would have been too upfront, so I chose an excuse I thought would disarm her. I reminded her that I needed it for a very important passage in my novel and that I couldn't continue until I had cleared that snag. It was a serious thing, creative work was like that, you got obsessed with one word and got stuck and couldn't go on no matter how great an effort you made. As she still didn't say anything, I worked on this idea—perhaps too long. I hinted that I wanted her to appear in the novel as a character. Still, she said nothing. "What do you think?" I finally asked.

The following three or four seconds seemed endless. "What do you want me to say? That it fills me with admiration?" She was very harsh. She said she really admired the way I profited from my literary production, and hoped the words that had seduced her would also be to the critics' taste. "The words that seduced me," was exactly how she put it.

"The thing is, I need it," I wailed. And I wasn't pretending; however regrettable it was, I really did need that text. I mustered all my boldness and reminded her that she had promised to send it. In fact, she didn't have to bother sending it by mail; if she would only read it out slowly, I could jot it down.

"Didn't you get my letter?"

I was taken aback, and, realizing that she had already sent the note, mourned my lost dignity. No, I hadn't received anything. Well, she had taken it to the post office a couple of days ago, so I would get it soon. I would have preferred her to read it aloud again, but I didn't suspect anything untoward. I was convinced that I'd get my note in a few days.

"Now you'll have to excuse me, I've got a lot of work to do."

She didn't give me time to say goodbye; she simply hung up. It didn't upset me, though. I didn't care about anything Eugenia did or said. I searched the house from top to bottom, looking for a cigarette; smoking helps me cope with anxiety. This kept me occupied for a while, until, in the pocket of a winter jacket, I found a pack I had hidden there, almost unconsciously, for precisely such an occasion. I've sometimes asked myself whether having made anxiety an excuse to smoke has increased the number of situations in which I feel anxious. But it's hard to stop that vicious circle.

So from the moment Eugenia hung up, I spent the day smoking one cigarette after the other. I neither ate nor slept. On the following morning I kept going down to my mailbox every ten minutes to check if the postman had left anything for me. He finally turned up at one o'clock. I think I gave him a fright when I emerged from the half-light of the porch, unshaven, wearing a gabardine over my pajamas.

He gave me three or four envelopes, one of which (blue, scented) was Eugenia's. I dropped the others and opened Eugenia's. The paper was the same color as the envelope, and the text, written in ink, ran as follows:

Darling,

If you want your note back, which in fact is mine (ours?), come to the hotel El Palacete, on Serrano Street, on Wednesday the 26th at nine o'clock in the evening.

Ardently yours, Eugenia.

P.S. If you agree, leave a message in my office early that day. Don't bother trying to get in touch with me before then. I'll be away.

In my state—agitated, lighting a cigarette every ten minutes since my relapse—I was unable to interpret Eugenia's behavior as a game. I even thought about picking up the phone and telling her to stop messing around, that I was very busy and that I wanted her to read the text, slowly, so I could take it down once and for all. But on second thought I decided it was too risky. She might get angry. I considered buttering her up with tender words: I would implore her to read me the note (in my anguish, it wouldn't take much to start crying, even) and tell her I would go to Madrid later, when I was in better spirits. But I couldn't do this either, because when I finally found the courage to call, her secretary told me she was away, as she had warned.

My only choice, therefore, was to accept her conditions. I had to go to Madrid. But I still had five days until the 26th. I called Sedano and told him I was very nervous because I had sent a novel to a literary competition and the result was imminent. I don't know why I used that excuse instead of any other, because he got quite worked up about my having sent the novel without showing it to him. He told me that sending novels to competitions amounts to literary prostitution. In any case, I was only able to get one vial of valiums out of him.

The following five days, which I spent swallowing two valiums with a shot of Armagnac every two hours, are completely blank. I can't remember what I did. On the 26th, early in the morning, I left a message at Eugenia's office saying that I accepted her conditions. I then took a double dose of valium and went to the Norte train station. I didn't want to take the afternoon train, because I feared that any accident or unexpected event might make me late for my date on Serrano Street.

The lifestyle I had led in the last five days—confined to my house, consuming nothing but valium and alcohol, smoking one cigarette after another, dozing but never really giving myself up to sleep—had left me looking scruffy. My skin was ashen and yellowish, the color of nicotine; I had sunken eyes and cracked lips. To look a little more decent, I stopped taking the pills, drank only coffee and water on the journey, and found the willpower not to smoke a single cigarette.

The first thing I did when I got to Chamartín was take a room at the hotel and lie down on the bed. I was sure that Eugenia's little game was designed to reproduce the scene I'd described in my note, and I considered following the script and buying a bottle of champagne, but in the end I didn't, partly because I wasn't in the right mood, but above all because I wanted to make it clear that all I was after was the note.

I had a remote and fragmentary recollection of making love in that same hotel two years before. No doubt it hadn't been momentous; her passion had intimidated me and I had the impression that it was precisely my shyness that excited her. Also, there was something about the intimacy of her naked body I found unpleasant. I couldn't remember what she looked like naked, probably because I had tried not to look at her. I knew that the odds of getting away without having sex with her that night were very slim, in fact hopelessly stacked against me, but I kept telling myself that with some luck she wouldn't dare propose it. To be completely honest, I feared that once the moment came I'd be unable to play my part with dignity; I felt very weak.

Lying there in the darkness I felt like a boxer before a fight, trying to mobilize his strength and calm his nerves. But I had someone to offer my sacrifice to, and this thought guided me into a peaceful state in which the images I cherished most tamely obeyed my call. I fell asleep as I imagined Victoria reading my manuscript on the Normandy beach. Now and then I half woke with the following sequence in my mind: Victoria stretching out her arm, me answering the phone, the short crescendo in the *Pavana*, then the diminuendo, fading into the piano… "It's wonderful," she said as I drifted into a deeper sleep…

Until the brain-splitting sound of a horn woke me up. I felt as if someone had shattered an entire tea set in my head. The room was totally dark. Still unable to move a muscle, my first task was to identify the noise coming from outside. They were Real Madrid supporters going from the Chamartín train station to the stadium, shouting, "*Madrid, Madrid.*" Suddenly, as I became conscious of where I was, I realized I barely had time for a quick shower if I was to make my date with Eugenia.

I had problems finding a taxi, but luckily the traffic moved swiftly down Castellana Street to the city center.

Not so in the other direction; there was a crowd going to
the soccer stadium shouting, "*Ala Madrid*." From time to
time I also saw some blue and white flags, and even one
or two *ikurrinas*.* The taxi driver confirmed that Real
Madrid was playing Real Sociedad.

I arrived at the hotel five minutes ahead of time. It's
at the end of Serrano Street where the villas are, and as
Victoria had told me, it's very pretty and quiet. The lobby
looks like a bourgeois living room, with its floral sofas and
armchairs and dimmed floor lamps. Before I finished saying my surname, the middle-aged woman behind the
counter told me: "*Su señora está en la 12.*"

I thought calling Eugenia my wife was taking discretion a bit far, but I didn't sense any sarcasm in the
woman's tone. The floor in the corridor was smoothly car-
peted and the paintings on the wall seemed good. Perhaps
Victoria had sold them to the hotel. I didn't have to wait
long in front of room 12. Exactly ten seconds, in fact, for
I had started counting when I knocked on the door, and
with all the practice I've had I'm as accurate as a Swiss
clock. Eugenia was wearing her suede jacket. "*Pasa*," she
told me.

The room was nearly dark. Through the wide window I could see the black elms outside playing with the
cobalt-blue twilight sky. We didn't kiss, and shaking her
hand seemed too cold. I said, "*Hola*," and then, "Long
time no see!"

"Yes, long time no see."

Trying to avoid her eyes, I glanced around the room.
It was decorated in the English style. There was a desk, a

---

* Real Sociedad is San Sebastián's soccer team; its colors are white and
blue. *Ikurrina* is the name of the Basque flag. (T.N.)

sofa, two armchairs that might have been cream-colored, and behind a curtain, the foot of a bed. A gentle bone-colored light emanated from behind the curtain. This, then, was the sort of atmosphere Victoria liked.

Eugenia still hadn't taken off her jacket. She went to the desk, took out an envelope from the drawer and gave it to me. It was one of her blue, violet-scented envelopes. I grabbed it quickly; too quickly perhaps. Even from the most optimistic viewpoint, and I had considered many, was I really to believe that I'd get my note back so quickly and with such little effort? I wasn't bold enough to check the contents—I hate the kind of distrustful people who count the change you give them—so I stood there with the envelope in my hand, not knowing what to do. I regretted not having kissed her when I came in, and wanted to compensate her for my tactlessness, but could only repeat, "Long time no see!" And then, "More than a year."

"Nineteen months since you did me the favor of fucking me in a station hotel."

I would have preferred a slap in the face. I had to shake my head not to pass out. Instinctively I looked at the envelope. The time had come to overcome my scruples and check its content. It was she, however, who ordered me to.

"Open it," she said.

As I was tearing the envelope, she disappeared into the back room. The sheet inside the envelope was also blue. It clearly wasn't the note I'd written, nor was it a copy. It was a different text, written in ink, in big clear handwriting:

What you desire is in me, between my lips, on my tongue, on my pink palate; it is in my eye, enclosed in its warm eye-

lid, gushing, shining, moistening; and you have to recover it with total innocence, that is, denuded of everything, of clothes, of prejudices, and using only your lips.

I started to feel unwell. I can't say that at the time Eugenia's words (*gushing, shining, moistening* eye) reminded me of Monique Wittig's periphrastic description of the feminine sex in *Les Guérrilliéres*, a book Eugenia had recommended to me when it came out, but I swear I'd never been so frightened.

I didn't know what to do. I could see her through the corner of my eye, sitting on the edge of the bed having already taken her jacket off. I wanted to strangle her, but felt incapable of it. Besides, I wouldn't be able to do it quickly enough to prevent her from shouting. I drew nearer, toward the curtain that separated the living room from the bedroom. The walls looked more ochre in there, probably because of the bed lamp's mellow light. On them hung several collages with blue figures that resembled Matisse's. I had the same thought as before: I was in an environment that would suit Victoria, but Eugenia was the one sitting on the edge of the bed.

I decided to say that I understood nothing. I spoke to my reflection in the mirror above the dresser. "I don't understand a thing," I said. "Really, I don't understand a thing."

"You don't understand a thing."

She only repeated my words, perhaps to show pity, boredom, exhaustion. I asked myself if the fear that she would start to shout was what really prevented me from strangling her. Anticipating her piercing cries was making me stay there, fists clenched in my pockets, restraining myself from pouncing on her. I had to count to ten. That's

what Sedano used to tell me: whenever I felt nervous I
should count to ten before saying anything. So while she
murmured, "You don't understand a thing" (she said it
five or six times, her tone growing more pitying), I repeated the exercise of counting to ten three times.

In the end my hands relaxed and the pain I had felt
in my chest disappeared. I felt like kneeling at her feet and
begging her to give me the note back, because I was in
love with Victoria. I don't know what she would have
done. I have the impression that women respect this kind
of thing even when they don't understand it, or perhaps I
should say they forgive them. But I couldn't confirm this,
because I didn't tell her anything. It was she who spoke:

"You don't have to understand," she said to the mirror. "You only have to act."

"What do I have to do?" I mumbled.

"Recover the marvelous text that you wrote for me
and that you've already forgotten."

I'm not sure there wasn't a slight mocking tone in her
voice. She had often told me she found it marvelous, and
I had completely trusted her.

I clenched my fists in my pockets again and asked her
what I had to do.

"First strip naked, like the sons of the sea."

"Well, if that's all," I said, feigning indifference.

I acted as if I had taken it to be a joke. I unbuttoned
my jacket as I hummed a tune, let it slip off my arms with
a coquettish shrug, swung it over my head and threw it at
her feet like a stripper. Nothing about her suggested she
found this remotely funny, and I felt ridiculous. "Pathetic" is the word.

She got up from the bed and unzipped her dress to
the waist. It was a sleeveless dress whose v-neck revealed

the white straps of her bra. I stepped back into the safer ground of the living room.

"Get undressed in the bathroom and tell me when you're ready."

She said it without any fuss, in a neutral tone; she showed no bitterness, but didn't seem to be joking either. It was like being told by a doctor, "Go in there and take off your clothes, please."

I went into the bathroom trying to convince myself that it was all a game, but I was scared. My hands were wet and my armpits gave off a strong smell of sweat. I stripped naked and washed my hands, armpits and head in the sink. My face looked pale and haggard under the raw white light. "I'm ready," I said, looking at myself in the mirror.

"You can come," she answered.

I walked out. In an effort to control my sense of shame, I tried to swing my arms in as natural a way as possible as I walked toward her. She was naked too, leaning against the headboard with her hands folded behind her head and her feet flat on the bed.

The most reasonable thing to do would have been to tell her that the whole business was absurd, to get dressed and leave, but I was obsessed with getting the note back. Indeed, if it had been powerful enough to bring Eugenia to this point, it had to work with Victoria, too. These premises being false, they were leading me to a false conclusion: that I needed the note to gain Victoria's love. I find it incredible now, but at the time I felt I wouldn't know what to tell Victoria without those words. Saying, "I love you," wasn't enough for me.

I stood at the foot of the bed with my hands crossed in front of me, fighting the temptation to cover my penis.

Seeing her from above, I had the impression that she looked somewhat bigger around the waist; I remembered her as thinner. Her breasts, too, looked quite full; perhaps raising her arms behind her head helped a bit. "Come on, give me that damned note," I wanted to tell her, but my voice failed me, and it was she who said, "Come on, come here."

I didn't move, for fear of what she might do to me if I got closer. I burn with shame to admit this, but I stood on my tiptoes and raised my arms over my head like a ballerina, once more trying to hide my true grotesqueness behind a comical pose. I took only one step, and was paralyzed again. "Don't play the fool," she told me, though she didn't have to say it, for I could read the contempt on her face. "Don't be pathetic," was another thing she might have said, for she often used that terrible word. I was indeed pathetic, standing there beside the bed, not knowing what to do. Finally I held out my arms and took one step forward like a blind man, thinking that she would extend hers too, bring the note out from under the pillow and give it to me. "Come and get your lousy literature," she said this time, actually moving her arms. But instead of giving me the note, she raised herself up on her elbows and spread her bent legs completely, nearly touching the bed with her knees. "Come on, take it," she said, lifting her buttocks. She moved her hips up and down several times, raising her sex at me and saying, "Come on, take it." It wasn't an invitation; it was something between a command and a challenge, and didn't lend itself to comic interpretation. I asked myself how I had managed to get into this situation, but felt incapable of recovering my long-lost dignity and getting out while I could.

I could have told her that that was enough playing around, but I felt unable to utter a word. I'm not sure whether my reason for remaining there, exposed to her, my teeth chattering (for suddenly my sweat had dried and I felt cold), was my desire to recover the note or simply that I couldn't do anything else. In any case I stayed there by the bed like a chastened child as she repeated, "Come on, take it" again and again. I don't know how much time passed—more than a minute, perhaps, enough to count to a hundred, in any case—before she finally held out her hand and I reached for it.

I had to put my knee on the edge of the bed. She took my hand and pulled me toward her. I meekly obeyed her, and nature also obeyed me giving me a decent erection, which was all I asked for.

"Take it," she repeated with terrible contempt in her voice, grabbing both my ears and pulling. But it was precisely her contempt that was making me hold back, even though it hurt. I closed my eyes to hide the tears and had a vision of myself swirling down a drain, surrounded by a whirlpool of images: black figures lit up by the candles they were carrying, the tombstones of Highgate Cemetery covered in weeds, the rusty gates of the crypts and the gray spider webs flapping in the wind and rain like thick flags of death. Images of the black wet ground, then an open grave, and at the bottom Lizzy Siddal as Beata Beatrix, covered from head to toe in her overgrown red hair, as in a funeral robe. Frizzy, electrified, burning hair. She was holding Rossetti's half-rotten poetry book against her breast, and the repulsive pink bird was pecking her hands, and her blood was splashing on me.

A pungent acrid smell filled my nostrils and I opened my eyes. There it was: the piece of paper I needed to con-

quer Victoria's love, sticking out of Eugenia's sex. The
larger lips were limp, but the small ones throbbed around
the paper cylinder, bright and red like the edges of an
open wound. She commanded me to take it, trying to pull
me toward her while pushing my shoulders down with her
feet. I didn't move. I couldn't do it, and I can't really
explain why. Maybe it was disgust, or fear, I don't know. I
remained lying face down on the bed. Whenever I raised
my eyes I saw her bloody wound in front of me: the glis-
tening, gushing eye, that cephalopod mouth looking at
me from between its open lips.

I backed away. I had no scruples about using all my
strength to get rid of Eugenia, and finally got out of the
bed. Without turning my back on her completely, I started to move away. Leaning back on her elbows, she followed me with eyes that reflected curiosity more than anything else. As soon as I crossed the curtain, I ran for the
bathroom.

I wet my face and dressed as quickly as possible. Having done so, I felt more relaxed. I leaned over the sink and
examined my face in the mirror. It looked haggard, yes,
pale, and more so with my hair wet. But the image of my
face arrested me, maybe because I noticed something in it
that I hadn't seen until then, or because I was used to
looking at it without really seeing it. For the first time in
my life, I asked myself whether I might not in fact be a
miserable wretch; that is, whether my impulses, my feelings, which until then I had considered normal, might not
be those of a base person.

Perhaps being base, which was such a terrible thing
for Victoria (I can still recall in every detail the look on
her face when she called Rossetti a wretch), was my normal state. Looking at my own image in the mirror, I

promised myself that I would try not to be a wretch from that moment on.

I felt better. There was no sound behind the door. I did up the top button of my shirt and walked out. I confess that, as I was coming out of the bathroom, I still considered going back into the bedroom and taking the note from her by force, but didn't. I was afraid she might attack me—I admit it. I closed the bathroom door behind me and took the time to count to ten before crossing the living room, making as little noise as possible. Though I tried not to look in the direction of the bedroom, I caught a glimpse of her sitting on the edge of the bed, holding something—perhaps the sheet—against her breast.

I was already in the corridor when I heard her voice. It wasn't a shout, but a question, asked in a normal tone: "Where are you going?" Instead of turning back and telling her there was nothing to keep me there, I kept walking, quickly but without running, a little less agitated now, for I knew that, being naked, she wouldn't be able to follow me. I was telling myself I had nothing to worry about, when I caught sight of Victoria at the end of the corridor. She seemed to emerge from the ground as she mounted the stairs.

She opened her arms in an effusive gesture. "You here! What a nice surprise!" she said, stopping at the top of the stairs.

I also stopped, trying to find an excuse that would justify my having to leave the place as soon as possible, for Eugenia might appear at any second. So we stopped at a distance of some feet apart and she said again, "What a surprise!" I decided that all I could do was tell her that we had to leave, take her by the arm and lead her downstairs, saying I would explain later.

Just then I noticed Victoria's bewildered eyes focusing on something behind me, and heard Eugenia shouting, "Where are you going, you wretch! You forgot this!" As incredible as it may seem, she used that exact word. I assume she was holding out my note, rolled into a tube. I don't know if she was naked, because I didn't look back. I didn't look at Victoria either. I just raced down the stairs and, once outside, ran down the whole of Serrano Street and into the Barrio de Salamanca district, until I realized people might take me for an escaping thief and stopped running. But I kept on walking at a fast pace until I got to Alcalá. There, with Retiro park in sight, I calmed down, probably because I was in a place I was more familiar with.

In former days, half the population of San Sebastián, myself including, stayed at the Alcalá Hotel. Muguruza was assassinated there and Esnaola was badly hurt. The Baroja family also lived there, around the corner, on Alfonso XII Street. The memories brought back by the familiar landscape soothed me a bit, and I was able to think, though in a rather disordered way.

I was happy that I had managed to get out of such an unpleasant and difficult situation, but I realized that what had happened would have serious consequences. The most serious one was that I'd never be able to look Victoria in the face again. In the light of this insight, I decided not to try to make up any excuses to justify myself. I wouldn't, for instance, blame Eugenia for everything that had happened, though that was the first thought that came to mind—telling Victoria I didn't know why that hysterical woman had attacked me.

I had to behave like an adult, as Sedano used to tell me: face reality. And reality was that Victoria had seen me in a disgraceful situation, being pursued by Eugenia, who was probably naked (she couldn't have had time to get dressed), shouting, "Where are you going, you wretch!" And even the most perfect excuse couldn't undo that.

I decided I had to stop thinking; I would take a taxi to my hotel and switch on the television, because it never fails to make me doze off.

When I arrived at Chamartín, instead of going directly to the hotel, I went to the station to have a cup of coffee and buy a pack of cigarettes. Sedano says that even if he smokes two packs on a given day, he can stop whenever he wants. According to him addiction is a consequence of Christianity. He argues that if people relapse into addiction once they have broken a period of abstinence by having one cigarette, it's because they are following Christian logic, which makes no distinction between committing one sin or twenty a day. There's no doubt that this Christian awareness of sin is deeply rooted in me, but I don't think Sedano himself is as liberated as he likes to think. And in any case, ever since the telephone-tapping affair, he's been on forty a day.

I consulted the timetable to check whether I still had time to catch the night train, but the idea didn't seem inviting, because I can't sleep in those sleeping compartments, and traveling by train at night causes me considerable distress. The ghostly light of the stations where the train stops, and the time it takes to pull away again! The echo of that metallic sound when the attendants strike the wheels with iron bars to check their strength. The ghostly voice announcing, "Last call for the passengers on the train to Irún," and the voices and footsteps coming in from the corridor, continually menacing the already fragile privacy of the compartment. So I smoked several cigarettes without really feeling bad about it, for almost everyone smokes in stations at night, and those who don't aren't

really bothered about the smoke. I also ate some deep-
fried pastry with my coffee (cold and greasy, as usual) and
noticed I wasn't the only one. There must be something
about the Madrid climate that makes people immune to
the dyspeptic effects of cold deep-fried fat.

We (those of us who had nothing better to do at night
than sit in a train station) looked like the soldiers of a
defeated army, quite desolate among the station's modern
facilities, and uncomfortable under the intense light. A
woman approached me, showed me a piece of paper with
a phone number written on it, and asked me to help her
make the call. She said she couldn't make out the num-
bers. She was one of those women who look a lot older
than they are, probably because of their old-fashioned
clothes and hairstyles. It's amusing that in the era of satel-
lite communication this kind of con to avoid paying for
long-distance calls is still being used. But the truth is that,
once you've helped them to the phone, you have to be
very miserly not to use your own coins.

They also tell you how lonely they feel, all alone in a
big city, and how sad their lives are. I helped the woman
to the phone box, dialed the number and gave her my
spare change, without daring to tell her that I felt alone
too. Then I went outside. In the street there was a group
of Real Sociedad fans holding their white and blue flags,
even though there wasn't a breath of wind in Madrid to
stir them. Looking at the fans, it was quite unnecessary to
ask about the outcome of the match. Nevertheless, I
asked. They'd lost 1–4, but they'd been robbed. I felt sorry
for them, sorry that something that left me so indifferent
made them so upset. But I also felt envious, for I supposed
it meant they didn't have more important problems to
worry about.

I only had to cross the taxi lane to get to the hotel. As I've said, that's the advantage of railway hotels—because they are right by the railway, they are, so to speak, on the way home. They allow people who dislike traveling to always feel at home, even when crisscrossing the globe. This is true in my case, except for the days I spent with Victoria in London; I was happy there, I didn't feel home-sick, nor did I feel the need to be near the railway.

I peered into the hotel lobby from outside, fearing Eugenia might be there, lying in wait for me, for she knew I usually stayed at the Chamartín. I didn't see her, but when I asked for my key the receptionist handed me a message: "9:45. Eugenia. Just to say goodbye."

The note gave no indication that she intended to call again, much less that she might appear at the hotel, but I was nevertheless fearful when I got into bed, after having twice checked that my door was locked. I hardly slept that night; whenever I started to feel drowsy, my imagination formed humiliating images, probably because fatigue was affecting my will and also because I secretly wanted to punish myself.

Eugenia's image appeared to me again and again: she was lying on a bed, naked, and after lewdly reaching between her thighs she took out a roll of paper and threw it at me saying, "Take your shitty literature," while I went for it on all fours, like a dog. I could actually feel the sour moisture on the paper. Finally, near dawn, my body sur-rendered to sleep, those images still in my mind, and when I awoke it was already time for me to leave for the airport.

On the way, my anxiety that Eugenia might be wait-ing for me reappeared. She would easily be able to guess that, since I hadn't left on the night train, I would take the first plane in the morning. Waiting in the queue to check in, I wondered what would be worse: having to confront Eugenia once more, or never seeing Victoria again. I'm a coward, but not to the point of hiding my cowardice from myself, and I admit that at that moment I would readily have accepted never seeing Victoria again in exchange for not having to face Eugenia. Anything other than being told, "Take your shitty literature" in front of other people. Nevertheless, I repeated to myself that if I ever found myself in that situation again, no matter what she said about my writing I wouldn't leave without getting hold of my note.

So it seems I was still interested in retrieving my note. I can't explain why. Perhaps I still saw it as a talisman that could help me conquer Victoria. Either that or I believed it had genuine literary value. That is, I considered it worth publishing. No need to say that, at the time, I believed Eugenia's humiliating remark had been spoken out of pure resentment, because she had guessed that I had wanted the note for someone else, not because she had lied to me when she described how deeply it had affected her. I was still convinced that the only reason why Eugenia had wanted to go to bed with me was that I'd been able to write a text she thought was wonderful. I couldn't see that any text, good or bad, would have had the same effect on her, as long as it had been written by me, or rather, *for her*.

And of course I still also believed that if I were given the opportunity to send the same note to Victoria, it would be a success with her too. Human beings adapt to all kinds of situations; that is at once their greatness and their baseness. I confess that the fact that Victoria had witnessed the pathetic scene at the hotel on Serrano Street hadn't killed my hopes of rectifying the situation.

"You won't believe it. You won't believe what an absurd thing has happened to me," I would tell her. I would choose that common expression to begin with (besides, it was the only thing I could think of) and then improvise as I went along.

Anyway, I decided not to think about that for the time being, believing that if I forgot about it something would unexpectedly come to mind; as I've said, in my experience this is exactly what tends to happen, not only with memories but also with ideas.

As I approached the gate, the loudspeakers announced that my flight was delayed. There were many people in the lounge, most of whom had nothing better to do than stare at the newcomer, and, as I usually do when I feel observed, I sat in a corner and hid behind a book.

She was right in front of me. I saw her as soon as I abandoned my self-imposed quarantine and looked up. She was wearing an elegant suit and sitting with her long legs crossed. Beside her was a man who might very well have been the one who had waited for her outside the hotel in London, and who in any case was equally elderly and refined. I didn't move. She must have seen me when I came in, but she had remained motionless until our eyes met. Then she simply got up. She stood beside her chair, looking at me. I saw no anger in her eyes. I have since come to believe that this was precisely the worst thing. At the time, however, what I optimistically considered the neutral look on her face encouraged me to approach her.

"*Hola*," I said.

"*Hola*," she replied. The man beside her looked up and she introduced us. "My director, Mr. Marleen," she said in English. As he got up, the man said, "As in Lili," and laughed. His laughter was extravagant, like his

teeth—too perfect to be real. He probably always said that
when he was introduced to someone. Then Victoria introduced me, adding that I was an expert in Dante Gabriel
Rossetti. Not knowing how to take it, I protested so he
wouldn't think she was serious.

In any case, he didn't seem too intimidated to offer
his opinion to an expert.

"Interesting, Dante Gabriel Rossetti. *Un fou des
femmes vraiment.*" When he said that he admired Rossetti
as a man and a painter, I looked at Victoria expecting her
to object, but she didn't say a word. I had the impression
that she wasn't really listening, as if it was all too familiar
to her.

Trying to sound clever, I ventured to reply that that
wasn't a universally held opinion, but he paid no attention
to me. He went on to say that what he found most attractive about Rossetti was his obsession with women.
Throughout his life, he had only painted women, and in
his later years only one: the queen of models, Jane Morris,
a hopeless love. He laughed again, displaying his perfect
set of teeth. "*N'est-ce pas?*" At some point he had stopped
speaking English and switched to French, thinking that
I'd understand him better, I suppose. He was fluent in
both languages.

He had a habit of saying "*n'est-ce pas*" after every sentence, and spoke very enthusiastically. I thought he might
be one of those libidinous old fans of Rossetti Victoria
hated so much, but what he said about Rossetti, though it
can probably be found in any art book, seemed curious to
me. He said that Rossetti's paintings, no matter what their
ostensible subject is, and even when they convey a specific literary theme, always speak of love.

"A painter can paint a portrait of the woman he loves, but in most cases it will remain merely a portrait; Rossetti's work, however, his endlessly painting the same face over and over again, testifies to his obsessive love."

Even though I would have liked to say something about the baser side of Rossetti's nature to please Victoria, I couldn't find the right moment. The way he continuously repeated "*n'est-ce pas*" compelled me to nod in assent, and I felt uncertain in the face of his verbosity. Perhaps I was glad he was praising Rossetti—the wretch—in front of Victoria, since to some extent he was thereby dignifying me. After all, it was my desire to win her love that had brought me to the hotel on Serrano Street in the first place, and I would have gone to Highgate Cemetery to open graves if necessary.

That was what I wanted to tell Victoria, but she had turned to look out the window. And I would also have lost myself in the unfailingly amazing spectacle of a plane taking off, had not the man touched my arm, wanting attention. He was asking what I did for a living. "I'm a writer," I said. He repeated it.

"Literature," he said, "is a testimony to love's power to make us sing or cry. The visual arts, on the contrary, are mute, and thus their power to express feelings is limited. For that reason, whereas poets of love are relatively common, painters of love are not easily found." He put a hand on my shoulder and stuck out his index finger. "If I had to name a painter of love, I would say Dante Gabriel Rossetti."

"Dante Gabriel Rossetti," Victoria said, turning from the window. She said it with a note of pity, of weariness. "*Ah oui, je connais bien votre opinion.*"

They both laughed, and I did the same, though I didn't know why. Then we fell silent for a moment, which seemed long and uncomfortable, until the loudspeakers called us aboard. We went to the gate together. Victoria walked between the man and me.

"I didn't expect to see you," she said in Basque.

I replied that I hadn't expected to see her either. The man said, "*C'est agréable quand vous parlez votre langue,*" and walked ahead of us to the bus.

It was true that I hadn't expected it, though I had wished for it. I could have told her that; it didn't seem too bold. However, I reckoned that before saying anything else I had to explain the events of the previous night. That was probably what she was waiting for. But apart from, "You won't believe it," I couldn't think of anything to say. It seems so easy now. I could have said I wanted to tell her everything that had happened, but that I needed more time, that I would explain everything to her in San Sebastián if she would agree to meet me somewhere for a cup of coffee.

But I was unable to add a single reasonable thing to, "You won't believe it." I felt as though I were poised at the top of a steep ski slope; I wanted to say, "You won't believe it" and let myself go, but at the same time I was frightened of receiving a curt reply. I broke into a sweat just thinking that she might answer, "You're right, I won't." So I only told her that I hadn't expected to see her either.

"But, since you're here," she said, opening her bag and taking out a parcel that clearly contained books, "I've been carrying them all week. I've been meaning to send them." She gave me the parcel. I tore open the paper and started leafing through the books, but she stopped me. "Not now," she said. "I've written you some lines, but I don't know if they make any sense now." She shook her head as if to oust her thoughts and said, "Anyway, I feel embarrassed now."

I thanked her.

We said nothing the whole way from the terminal to the plane. Several times I was about to tell her, "You won't believe it." I even found something else to say: "Everything I've done, I've done for your love." That sentence more or less captured the essence of what had happened, but I think I still entertained hopes of finding more appropriate words, as well as a more suitable occasion to say them. Besides, I was very eager to read her note, in part to find out how to proceed without putting myself in jeopardy.

We were already queuing for the plane. "Well..." she said, and I had the impression that she was looking at the Englishman. "Well," I said. It was obvious that she intended to say goodbye then and there, and that when we landed at the airport in Hondarribia we wouldn't speak again.

"Who knows where we'll meet next."

She said it with a smile. She raised her right hand slightly, then let it drop again. I didn't pull mine out of my pocket.

"See you," she said.

I stayed behind while she joined the man at the front of the queue. He raised his hand in farewell, and so did I. Their seats were at the front of the plane, in business class; mine was at the very back, by the toilets. They barely showed any sign of recognition when I walked past. The man lowered his head and said "Bye," and I did the same.

As soon as I sat down I opened the parcel. There were two books: one was a collection of London photographs

which included several texts written by famous writers
who had lived there—Virginia Woolf, Henry James,
Dickens, Defoe, Verlaine and many more. It was entitled
London: Literary Walks. The other was *The Pre-Raphaelites*,
by Timothy Hilton. Having checked that each book had
a dedication written on its first page in large, clear handwriting, I postponed reading them, mostly to prolong the
feeling of excitement, but also because I was afraid to discover Victoria's message.

I had a look at the photographs in the first book. To
my surprise, the book chronicled the walks we had taken
together in London as accurately as if we had used it as a
guide. I was sure, however, that we had chosen most of the
places at random. Nevertheless, there they were: South
Kensington underground station, with its southern market touch; one of the memorials at Highgate, a stone angel
emerging from the weeds with its index finger on its lips;
the facade of Hotel 169 on the corner of Old Brompton
and Dryton; and many other places which seemed less
surprising in a guide to London, for instance the National Theatre, where we first met, Hyde Park, Regent's Park
and St. James Park, all of which are musts for tourists in
London. For me, however, coming across all these photographs was a wonderful coincidence.

"*Je n'oublierai jamais nos promenades dans Londres,*"
read the inscription.

The other one, on the title page of the essay about the
Pre-Raphaelites, read: "*J'espère pour toi que tu n'auras pas à
emprunter des mots, comme ton Rossetti.*"

I tried not to cry, but I couldn't hold back the tears.
She hoped I wouldn't need to steal words, like Rossetti. I
held the book open and pretended to read so my neigh-
bor wouldn't notice the state I was in. The book had many

illustrations of Rossetti's paintings, but I was captivated by *Beata Beatrix*.

The painting is beautiful, sad and very unsettling because of the way it blurs the borderlines between pleasure and suffering, between sexual and mystical ecstasy. If I'm not mistaken, the author, Timothy Hilton, claims that dismissing the painting as necrophilic is far too simplistic. He argues that *Beata Beatrix* is a declaration of love for a dead person and that because we find that kind of love painful, we tend to reject it.

Having read this, I suddenly felt the need to clarify two points, or rather to locate them in the course of events. The first was whether Victoria had written the dedications before or after the incident in the hotel on Serrano Street. That one I resolved quite quickly; I wanted them to have been written after she had seen me in that shameful situation—with Eugenia following me, probably naked—because that would mean she hadn't ascribed much importance to the incident. But for some reason it seemed unavoidable that she had written them before. My second doubt, as I was looking at *Beata Beatrix*, was whether Rossetti had painted it before or after Siddal's corpse had been dug up. I found the answer in the book: he had painted it before. I wanted it to have happened after, that is, I wanted the painting to have been the result of Rossetti's repentance for having desecrated Siddal's grave, but it wasn't so. Siddal died in 1862, Rossetti painted *Beata Beatrix* in 1863, and the body was exhumed in 1869.

The book reproduces a note Rossetti wrote to A. Charles Swinburne, in which he attempts to justify having taken legal steps to open the grave:

No one so much as herself would have approved of my doing this. Art was the only thing for which she felt very seriously. Had it been possible for her, I should have found the book on my pillow the night she was buried; and could she have opened the grave, no other hand would have been needed.

The truth is that when the poems were published after having been recovered from Siddal's grave, they were harshly criticized. In 1871, Robert Buchanan devoted some humiliating words to Rossetti in his famous pamphlet "The Fleshly School of Poetry," and in 1872 the painter tried to kill himself by drinking a flask of laudanum, as his wife had done.

But sometimes even death rejects us. Rossetti stopped looking after himself and, according to the book, the once lively and gallant man turned into a disgusting recluse. He spent his last years locked in his house in Cheyene Walk, Chelsea, surrounded by all types of animals—owls, marmots, kangaroos, parrots, raccoons—while he took delight in his decay. Dying did not come easy to him. Though he was taking 180 grams of chloral hydrate a day, as well as morphine, brandy, whisky and red wine (which he drank by the gallon), he lived until 1882. He drew his last breath on the 9th of April of that year. Highgate Cemetery refused to bury him, and he therefore lies in Burchington Churchyard, in Kent.

It's obvious that our own sufferings don't exempt us from responsibility for the pain we cause others, even if we—especially men—often feel inclined to think so. We tend to think that, since we suffer ourselves, we should be forgiven for making others suffer. It seems to us that the criminal who feels pain while provoking it, and can thus say, "Look how I'm suffering too," has the right to put himself on the same level as the victim. Because in our Christian culture suffering is said to purify the soul, we tend to believe that the criminal who repents and suffers is not truly wicked, at least not as wicked as he who takes pleasure in committing the crime, and that he therefore deserves better treatment. That's what Sedano says. He also says that, in any case, he would rather be wronged by an honest criminal than suffer doubly at the hands of a crafty wretch.

I believe that more and more women are inclined to agree with Sedano, and it seems to me that what they want above all are men who won't hurt them, no matter whether they are short, ugly or fat—especially if they can dance the bolero. I also think that women don't give a damn if that means that those men don't even have the minimum inner life that suffering requires. I understand all of that; I'm not a blind defender of romantic love. But I'm not indifferent to suffering either, and I feel sorry for Rossetti, because he mostly harmed himself.

After having read the book, I would have liked to talk about it with Victoria, to try to alter her low opinion of Rossetti, at least a little. After all, I imagined that whatever she thought of him, she might also think of me. If she considered Rossetti a wretch, she must think the same of me. I was brooding on these thoughts when the pilot announced that we were about to land in Hondarribia.

Landing frightens me. Not as much as taking off, but still quite a lot. Trying to control my fear, I repeated to myself that in any case I needn't worry much, since without Victoria's love, life had no meaning for me anyway. But it didn't help. No doubt this was because my base instinct for survival is more powerful than any noble feeling in me. As I was pondering all this, however, I began to think that perhaps all was not lost and that life was still worth living after all. And suddenly I saw the light. At certain times in life you see things anew in a flash and can't understand how you could have been so blind. The fact was that Victoria's dedications had been written before the incident on Serrano Street, but, and this was what really mattered, she had given them to me after, which meant that she hadn't taken back her words. She hadn't forgotten our walks in London.

This thought made me extremely happy, happier than ever before. The plane landed, the engines stopped, and I remained in my seat until the last passengers had left. I didn't want to encounter Victoria and find myself forced to say a hurried farewell in front of everybody, just like that. As my only luggage was my handbag, I headed toward the exit, stopped by the desk of a car rental company, and waited for Victoria to appear.

I didn't have to wait long. When I spotted her going outside with her elderly companion, I walked out and lingered by the door. I conspicuously looked at my watch several times, to indicate that I was waiting for somebody who was late. I hoped they would say goodbye to each other right there and go their separate ways.

It didn't happen. A big black car pulled up in front of them, and the driver took their luggage. I had to put an end to the suffocating apprehension I was feeling. I thought of approaching them, telling the man that it had been a pleasure and Victoria that I hoped to see her some day. But I decided to pretend I hadn't seen them, hoping she would come to me. I looked at my watch again and started to make gestures of irritation, shaking my head and clicking my tongue. When she approached me, she would undoubtedly ask me if there was a problem, and I would tell her that the friend who was to take me to San Sebastián hadn't turned up. Then she would naturally invite me to go with them, and with a bit of luck I would have the opportunity to get out of the car with her—if the two of them weren't going to the same place, that is. But I decided to reject this last possibility, because you can't carry out a plan successfully if you expect the worst from the start.

As I had hoped, Victoria did in fact approach me. I glanced at my watch yet again and shrugged my shoulders in a gesture of annoyance and despair. It didn't work, though. She didn't ask me what was wrong. She only said, "Goodbye," only that, and the word sounded more definitive than ever.

"I hope we'll meet again?" I said without much hope, and, reading her mind, added, "Someday…" with a smile. My lips hurt as if they'd been singed.

"Of course we will," she could have said, but she only said, "We'll meet again… someday." Then we fell silent. It's true that it was up to me to say something more definite, but I was in too much despair. In the end, I held out the books and ventured to say, "Thank you for your dedications," to which she replied, "As you see, I haven't written a postscript to them." It's clear to anyone who isn't a complete fool: her promise that she would never forget our walks in London no longer had any value.

The man was standing some feet away, holding the car door open. He forced a smile when he noticed that I was looking at him; so did I.

"Where's he from?"

I don't know why I asked that, but in any case she didn't answer. "Well," she said, turning to him and signaling that she was almost done. "Well, Juan Martin, good luck with the writing," for that's my name, Juan Martin, though everybody calls me Juan. I had told her in London that my grandfather had died when I was a teenager (he was already senile by then) and that I found him repulsive because he always smelled of urine. His name was Juan Martin and they named me after him. He was the only one who ever called me Juan Martin, and I hated it.

I had told her the story in Hyde Park, but she must have forgotten the most important part of the anecdote, for I'm sure she didn't mean to hurt me by calling me Juan Martin.

"I hope you get a lot done," she said. I simply answered, "I'll try."

What a precise expression: "My heart is in pain." That's what I would have liked to have told her at that moment—that sometimes one suddenly understands the true meaning of certain words and that this might precisely be the gift of poets. I'm sure she felt sad too. She raised her hand and wiggled her fingers. We said no more. She walked to the car, repeated the gesture, and they simply pulled away.

I had to wait a while for a taxi to turn up. I dozed the whole way home, my mind a blank, and didn't notice that we were in San Sebastián until the driver asked me if I liked the Kursaal auditorium. They had recently opened a delicatessen under the main building. That's another paradox of our culture: a shop selling stuffed peppers is considered more appropriate for an auditorium than a sound archive, for instance.

When I told the driver I thought the building was all right, he said, "Now see, *that's* beautiful," and nodded at the Victoria Eugenia Theater. The building is in front of my house, and what used to be a privileged view—for it is indeed one of the city's most beautiful buildings—has now become a punishment, uniting those two names, Victoria and Eugenia, in the very symbol of my misfortune.

I was brooding on this when the porter came up to bring me the novel I had lost in Paris so long ago, along with all my old mail. The manager of the Frantour hotel had written a cover letter in which he explained that they had found it in a completely unexpected place while renovating the offices, and that they were very sorry they hadn't been able to send it before. As I scanned the first pages of the manuscript, the whole novel suddenly flooded back into my mind in every detail. It's funny how memory works. I only needed to hold it in my hands to remember the note that the protagonist sends to the woman he desires, word for word.

I found the passage and checked whether my memory was accurate. There she was, the woman lying naked on the bed, her thighs burning, and the man with the two glasses in the pockets of his jacket, holding a bottle of champagne bedecked with pearls of water. There it was, the crap that had destroyed my life, and I couldn't understand how I had ever considered it good. I left it on the table and sank into my armchair, totally despondent.

It was obvious that instead of becoming obsessed with recovering those words, I should simply have told Victoria, "I cannot paint you, but I love you." The truth. After all, the most practical thing would have been to say what I really felt. But of course, <u>sometimes the truth is complicated and hard to express, especially when, like me, you're not a good speaker.</u>